# Sheltered in Haven

Quinley Dixon

Published by Quinley Dixon, 2020.

This is a work of fiction. Similarities to real people, places, or events are entirely coincidental.

SHELTERED IN HAVEN

**First edition. May 30, 2020.**

Copyright © 2020 Quinley Dixon.

Written by Quinley Dixon.

A portion of the proceeds of the Haven-on-the-Lake series will be donated to benefit those affected by COVID-19 who truly do deserve a Haven.

# GRACE

SATURDAY, APRIL 22
7:30 A.M.

GRACE DAWSON SITS ALONE in the airport parking lot with a surgical mask in her hands, feeling guilty for being grateful that she caught this awful disease.

*It's funny...*she thinks, as she runs her thumb and forefinger across the crisp, starched pleats...*how something that felt surreal to wear, just a few weeks ago, brings comfort to me now.*

Protective, familiar, and safe. Like a trusty childhood blanket. Grace isn't sure she's ready to go without it today.

Even though she's no longer contagious, has tested negative three weeks in a row, Grace still wears the mask in public. Because that's what she's supposed to do. Keeper of peace, follower of rules, model of the good example. Grace has always been that way. And now as a public figure, she feels even more compelled.

Well, *public figure* might be stretching her status and influence a bit. Sure, she's on television as a field reporter for her local news, but it's not like she's recognizable beyond her northern Michigan viewers. That's all about to change, though, once this story hits. Every network, social media, and streaming platform could be plastering her face across the globe by the time this week is out.

Her dreams are about to come true, while other people are dying. It's like a windfall of dirty money. But she has to do her job.

Grace knows she wasn't the first choice to cover the Haven story — or the second, or third, or hundred-and-twelfth. She just happens to meet the requirements that other reporters could not: She contracted the virus early and is now twenty-one days in the clear. A few other more seasoned pros might better fit the bill, but she supposes her looks and image are factors that worked in her favor.

Pretty but not artificial, in that girl-next-door kinda way, Grace is the sort of person that people talk to, confide in, and trust. She's a features reporter of the warm-fuzzy stuff that makes people say "aww" out loud.

Grace has a knack for listening in a way that makes the average Joe feel important. With deep concentration in her warm, brown eyes, she focuses on teachers and bakers and men-on-the-street with a look that says, "You matter." Add a laugh, a few tears, or sometimes, a hug, and the interview is topped with a bow.

Under other circumstances, Grace would fit right into Haven-on-the-Lake. But she knows she's not welcome today. Nor are the 250 others scheduled to arrive at the end of the week. Or the hundreds after that. The first wave, the second, and third of Immunity Community #1.

She has read the heated transcripts of phone calls between Mayor Ruby Irish and the politicians, officials, and experts that

Irish has talked to over the past few weeks. The mayor has been adamant about full disclosure, no secrets.

Ruby Irish has made it clear that Haveners are more than just a group of residents living in the same small city. They are family to each other — and to her. She wants them all to feel educated, respected, and prepared for the coming months ahead. If it's possible to prepare for this.

In truth, Grace feels bad for the people of Haven-on-the-Lake. They did everything right. They locked down their city long before anyone in North America had the foresight, or guts, to do so. Closed their docks, shut down their airport. No one came or left. They could have been protected for a very long time from any threat of this virus at all.

And now hundreds of people are moving into their town, by the President's command.

Grace compared this to the equivalent of strangers barging into her own home, touching her stuff, breathing her air, coughing on her food; contaminating her quarantine. How violating and invasive that would feel. Scary, shocking, wrong. *And, man, would she be pissed!* She could understand why Ruby Irish has been like a mama bear guarding her precious cubs.

And the fact that this Community was formed in response to the demands of the Survivors Freedom Alliance (SFA) doesn't help either. The folks on Haven probably think they're getting the worst of the Survivors: troublemakers, rebels and protesters.

That's how this whole thing started. One government protest in Lansing, Michigan, when the governor extended the shelter-in-place order, spread like wildfire across the country. Thanks to social media, the SFA grew to hundreds, then thousands, within a week. New protests were popping up everywhere. The White House couldn't ignore them anymore, even though the pandemic was getting worse.

Several countries were in full lockdown. American hospitals were overrun and understaffed. Personal protective equipment was scarce, as were ventilators and tests. Some cities didn't even have enough body bags, or space, for their dead. They were stacking the bodies in refrigerated trucks. And the U.S. death rate was still on its way up the spike.

Yet, SFA protests grew...and were now becoming dangerous due to lack of crowd control and the health risks of massive arrests. So, the President compromised, and announced what he claimed to be his own "brilliant" idea.

He announced that "America will be the first in the world to open isolated locations throughout the country that will be a hundred percent safe from the virus." Immunity Communities. Where those who have recovered from the virus could live and work and socialize without restriction, just as they did before the pandemic hit. These communities would serve as "beacons of hope to the world until we all unite even stronger than before."

Haven-on-the-Lake drew the unlucky straw to become Immunity Community #1.

GRACE IS ON HER WAY to cover Mayor Irish's first live broadcast from Haven this morning where she will introduce herself and her island to the world. Grace will be the first and only Survivor present, at the mayor's request. Ruby Irish has made it very clear that she doesn't want her residents to feel invaded. One reporter to cover the story was more than enough, she said.

The announcement is at 1 p.m. Grace's flight is at eleven. And she's been parked at the Fremont, Ohio airport since dawn. It took Grace two flights and a rental car to get to her closest access point to Haven-on-the-Lake, which sits in the middle of Lake Erie between Ohio and New York.

She had wanted to arrive on Haven the night before, but the island's only pilot had a previous engagement and couldn't make the trip until morning.

*A previous engagement?* Grace thought. *Who the hell has previous engagements anymore?*

She has to keep reminding herself that Haven is one of the few places in the world that has been living life normally all along. Of course, they have previous engagements! And dinner plans. And house parties. And hugs.

People walking around in masks six feet apart must seem as surreal to them as *not* worrying about the virus would feel to Grace right now.

Every day, she feels more of her pre-virus-self slipping away. Will she ever be comfortable in a crowd again? Shoulder to shoulder with strangers? Or even shaking someone's hand?

She is so glad she's no longer single and trying to date. Thank God for Michael.

As Grace watches the clock on the dashboard tick toward her departure time, she opens the files on her phone to research Haven and pass the hours.

GRACE HAD ONLY JUST been offered the assignment two days before, and she had to make the decision on the spot. She found out later that Julie Carr, from Chicago, was originally slated to go. But she had to cancel because her cough came back.

Of course, Grace jumped at the chance before she even ran it by her fiance'. Bill Carter, her producer, knew she had plans to get married this summer, but he had either forgotten or assumed the wedding was canceled. Grace figured she would deal with that later and make an excuse to go home sometime around late June.

The original wedding plan was for 200 guests to be dancing under the moonlight at a Sutton's Bay lakeside inn, the second weekend of July. Now they'll probably just have a small group of family and friends, most likely wearing masks, sitting at tables six feet apart. But Grace and Michael are committed to exchanging their vows, no matter where or how they do it.

In an effort to catch Grace up to speed for today, Bill sent her all the transcripts of the mayor's phone conversations so far and as many clips as he could find of her speeches, interviews, and live footage over the years. Which isn't much. But it's enough to see what Ruby Irish is made of.

Ruby has the intelligence, strength, and poise that naturally demand respect. She's very pretty, too. At 62, Ruby is fit and vibrant and chic. Her auburn hair is cut in a trendy, wavy bob and her tortoise-shell horn-rimmed glasses (like Grace has seen on Oprah) look both stylish and smart. She wears classic, casual clothes reflective of her small, charming town. And uses just the right amount of words to get the job done and get out.

In short, Ruby Irish has her shit together. And Grace hopes to make a good first impression. Being the first Survivor on the island is a lot of pressure.

As Bill told her before she left, "Irish says one reporter is enough to cover the first announcement. And you're the one. Make me proud." His lack of confidence in her was thinly veiled.

Grace had been determined to prove she was the right person for the job. She was poised, professional and prepared. And she could always get people to talk.

But with every tick of the clock, she doubted herself a little more.

IN TRUTH, GRACE DAWSON is the enemy. And what she needs to prepare for most is the very real possibility of being hated in Haven.

# THREE WEEKS EARLIER

OFFICIAL TRANSCRIPT
AUDIO CALL
SATURDAY, APRIL 1
7:30 a.m.
MAYOR RUBY IRISH,
HAVEN-ON-THE-LAKE
with U.S. VICE PRESIDENT
ROBERT PIERCE

**RUBY IRISH:** It's a simple question, Mr. Vice President. Can these so-called *Survivors* of the virus still be contagious?

**VICE PRESIDENT:** Well, I am not a doctor, Mayor Irish.

**IRISH:** Oh, I am *well aware* that you're not a doctor, or any type of medical expert whatsoever. But I would certainly hope you did a vast amount of research before proposing a plan to bring outsiders to the isolated island of Haven-on-the-Lake, which has been 100% protected from the virus so far. So, I am looking for a yes or no answer. Is it possible that any Survivors of the virus can still be contagious?

**VP:** Yes. There have been some inaccuracies in testing in which some Survivors have tested negative when they were actually positive. So, technically, yes, someone who was thought to be a Survivor could still be contagious. But...

**IRISH:** And what about secondary illnesses arising in the same person weeks after the initial symptoms have subsided? Is it possible a secondary illness could arise, weeks after testing negative? Yes or no, please.

**VP:** Yes. According to Mr. Gossi [CDC] this has happened with similar illnesses.

**IRISH:** Has it happened with this virus? Yes or no?

**VP:** Yes. There have been a limited number of individuals that have tested negative for this virus and then fell ill again weeks later with a different set of symptoms.

**IRISH:** Have any of those secondary illnesses been fatal?

**VP:** Not many. But yes.

**IRISH:** After supposedly fully recovering from the original virus?

**VP:** Yes.

**IRISH:** So, in a roundabout way, the cause of death was the original virus?

**VP:** Again, I am not a doctor. But, yes, the original virus would obviously be a factor.

**IRISH:** Therefore, they could still have been contagious during those asymptomatic weeks, even after testing negative for the virus. Yes or no?

**VP:** Again, I am *not* a medical expert, Mayor Irish, but, yes, I suppose that is possible.

**IRISH:** So on the basis of all of this information: Is it true — yes or no — that the so-called Survivors arriving on Haven, an island of 183 people who have been isolated, protected, and never exposed, could be bringing with them a contagious, deadly virus? A virus that could kill my people who otherwise could have avoided exposure for many more months, even years.

**VP:** Well, with all due respect, Mrs. Irish, they aren't *your* people. Haven-on-the-Lake is not a private island.

**IRISH:** Actually, I don't feel respected at all, *Mister* Pierce. And you and I both know Haven-on-the-Lake is completely self-sufficient. While seasonal tourism is our primary industry, there are six months every year that our residents do just fine without anyone else. Online businesses, remote employment and internal commerce are sufficient for us to survive years without anyone else setting foot on Haven, short of delivering essential supplies. Our pilot, Captain Gregory Finnegan, has been our sole supply source since November, without any direct human interaction and with extensive sterilization of the supplies. Therefore, we could remain isolated from this virus for as long as necessary, possibly until a vaccine is discovered. But you have decided to change all that by making us guinea pigs of your government experiment. You're sending hundreds of people who have been exposed to the virus to our perfectly healthy island in what you call *a message of hope*...to everyone but us. So, again, Vice President Pierce, is it possible that your *Immunity Community* could be a deadly threat to Haven-on-the-Lake?

**VP:** Well, it's not *my* communit...

**IRISH:** Could this **kill** my people, sir? YES OR NO?

**VP:** In the unlikely event that the virus is somehow transmitted, then yes, fatalities could result. But...

**IRISH:** Let the record show, Mr. Vice President, that the blood is on *your* hands.

**IRISH**: *motherfucker*

**VP:** Pardon?

RUBY THOUGHT SHE HAD disconnected the phone. But, honestly, she didn't care if the Vice President heard her.

She had much bigger things to worry about as she prepared to break the news to Haven.

# KADE

T*ime for...a co-oo-ool change. I know that it's time...for a cool change.*

Kade Irish has no idea how the Little River Band found their way to Rounds Bar, his humble little hole-in-the-wall on an island in the middle of nowhere. But he's awestruck as the lead singer, Glen Shorrock, belts out lyrics from his barstool.

*Now that my life...*

Kade, who happens to have his guitar behind the bar, starts strumming the chords like he wrote them. Totally nailing it.

*...is so prearranged...*

To his surprise, he rocks the vocals, too, sounding *exactly* like Glen.

*I know that it's time...for a coo-oo-ool change.*

Shrugging off Kara's poke to his shoulder, Kade has a flash of panic as he tries to remember the next verse. But Glen just circles back to the top of the chorus and they resume their duet.

*Ti-i-ime for...*

If only Kara would leave him alone! Couldn't she see this was a once-in-a-lifetime...

"Kade!" Kara says, sounding irritated...and raspy. "Your phone!"

*...a coo-oo-ool change.*

Kade's *Cool Change* ringtone rattles the cell phone on his nightstand. And, poof! Barstool Glen is gone.

"Dammit!" He says, frustrated at being forced to end his dream performance at...he picks up his phone...8:24 a.m. on a Saturday!

"Who the fuck...HELLO?!" Kade presses the phone to his right ear while rubbing his forehead with his left hand. Tequila hangovers are the worst.

This is why Kade only drinks in the off-season. Running a bar for fifteen hours a day in the hot summer would be brutal with a headache like this.

"Nice," Ruby Irish deadpans on the other end of the line. "Is that how I raised you to answer the phone?"

"Mom?" Kade says, wincing at the invisible ice pick piercing his right eye. The dirty bar rag smell of his own sweat makes his stomach turn. "What's wrong?"

"You mean besides the plague ravaging our world population and the global economy being flushed down the crapper?" Ruby says. "We've got a new problem, Son. I'm calling an emergency Town Hall this afternoon. At your bar. But I want our family there first. As soon as possible."

Kade feels the phone vibrate against his ear.

"I just sent a group text to your brothers and sister to be at the bar by ten," Ruby continues, now in full business-mode. "And Dottie and Frank will be there, too."

Awake, naked, and now sitting on the edge of his bed, Kade looks at last night's clothes puddled at his feet. The simple movement of his eyes sends another roiling wave of nausea through his gut and a fresh spear through his eyeballs.

"Wait. What. Hold on, Mom." Kade plucks his underwear off the floor and tosses his cell on the bed as he slips them on. Feels too weird to talk to his mom with his junk hanging out.

He grabs the phone and pads out of the room, closing the door behind him, careful not to wake Kara again. Or Crunch, who is snuggled at the foot of their bed, eyes half-mast, his yellow lab fur blending with the beige sheets.

"Did someone on the island test positive?" Kade asks.

"No," Ruby says. "But..."

She pauses and sighs, her exasperation sending an unsettling vibration through the airwaves.

Even after fifteen years as mayor, nearly half of Kade's life, this is out of character for his mother. If other women are their family's rock, Ruby would be Haven's mountain. Nothing rattles Ruby Irish.

"We have to let people in," she says. Quiet, weary, defeated.

"Whatta you mean, let people in. In where? My bar?"

"To the island. The government is making us open the island."

"Wait. What?!" Kade's burst triggers another sharp kick to his head.

It is *wa-a-a-ay* too early for this. Too early in the day. Too early in the pandemic. Too early for Haven.

"No fucking way!"

"Language," Ruby says, out of editorial correction more than motherly obligation. By no means a prude, Ruby has just always thought profanity to show a lack of creativity. *It's verbal laziness*, she's said, *when there are so many more colorful words to use.*

If Ruby herself ever drops the F-Bomb, you know you're in trouble.

"Seriously, Mom, they can't make us do that! We're the friggin' model of quarantine here. We're following their rules. We're safe! One positive case could wipe out our entire island. Oh, hell no!"

"I know, I know, I know." Kade can hear her rubbing her face.

"Listen, I don't want to go into this over the phone," she says, regaining composure. "I just got off a call with the Vice President and..."

"The Vice President *of the United States?*" Kade asks.

"No, Kade. Of the PTA," Ruby says. "Yes. Of the United States. They want to get people moving as soon as possible, which is why we need to make this announcement today."

"Jesus," Kade says.

He has questions. So many questions. But Kade has learned the limits of his mother's patience, as both a parent and a politician. And now is not the time to push them.

"Okay, what do you need me to do?"

"I need you to open the bar as soon as possible," Ruby says. "Don't tell anyone the details. Not even Kara, okay? I told Dottie and Frank to come early and start getting things set up while I meet with the family. I'm setting the Town Hall for two p.m."

"Okay," Kade says again. "Give me twenty minutes."

"Make it fifteen. Dottie and Frank are probably already there."

It wasn't even 8:30 yet.

Ruby Irish is in crisis control mode.

In contrast to her slim, sinewy frame (still a runner at 62) she has the steady, solid stance of a military general. She's also brilliant, with an intolerance for stupidity. Ruby doesn't waste time rehashing the details of what's been done or said. Instead, she focuses on what she can do next. What actions will best suit her city, her home, her family? She will do whatever it takes to protect her own.

Mayor Ruby Collins Irish would die for her Haven.

And Kade would be damned if he was going to let that happen.

# DOTTIE

Dottie and her husband, Buck, were the previous owners of Rounds Bar and ran it together for nearly fifty years before Buck sold to the Irishes. He'd fought and won two previous battles with cancer before Pancreatic finally took him out. Dottie thought of leaving Haven after he died, but there's no place in the world she loves more. And now, more than ever, she wishes Buck were here.

BENJAMIN EUGENE KESSNER (Buck to friends) was an island native.

In 1939, his father was hired as a chef at The Majestic, the island's biggest hotel, and his mother worked the reception desk. Buck was born a year later. He was their only child.

Even though The Majestic ("Madge" to locals) could have become a second home to young Buck, he never felt comfortable with the stiff formality of its palatial style. Buck much preferred to spend his time exploring the inland woods or hanging out at the docks to fish.

When Buck was twelve years old, he happened to plop down next to Alvin Wilson at Buffalo Pointe, a great place to catch Walleye in the spring. Alvin asked if Buck was old enough to work. The dishwasher at his bar had just quit and he needed someone right away. Apparently, twelve was good enough for Al and he asked Buck to show up at 10 a.m. the next day. Just then, Buck caught his biggest fish of the season, and he took it as a sign that he should say yes. Even though he had his reservations.

The only thing Buck knew about having a job was what he saw from his parents. And he didn't want any part of that never-home-always-tired-jump-when-your-boss-calls lifestyle. He told himself he'd give Mr. Wilson a week to find someone else and then go back to catching fish and being a kid.

But if The Majestic was Haven's queen, then Rounds Bar was the island's court jester.

The laid-back staff and salty clientele were on the other end of the spectrum from The Majestic's strict dress code and affluent guest list. Whereas mature adults vied to gain valuable work experience at the reputable hotel, Rounds Bar hired pretty partiers who weren't quite ready to grow up.

Rounds' small, greasy kitchen was filled with raunchy jokes, sweaty guys, and hot girls. The cavernous barroom boomed with lively tourists and seasoned locals who drank lots, laughed big, and stayed late. It was a colorful circus of harmless debauchery. And by the end of the first week, Buck felt like he'd found his people.

Alvin and Estelle Wilson, Rounds' original owners, never had any children of their own. And, over the years, as Buck soared up through the ranks of barback, bartender, then manager, the Wilsons found comfort in having someone else in the business they could trust. They involved Buck in more and more decisions, gave him increased responsibilities, and even took a vacation or two.

It was 1967, on the bar's 50th anniversary, when Alvin and Estelle announced their plans to retire to Florida. And then sold Rounds Bar to Buck Kessner for a song.

BUCK, A GOOD-LOOKING, likable guy with an easy smile, quick wit, and tireless energy was a natural in the service biz.

The fact that he inherited the best of his parents' French and Cherokee traits didn't hurt the bar's aesthetics either. Those who preferred Elvis were drawn to Buck's black hair and angular features, while Frank Sinatra fans commented on his dreamy blue eyes.

At twenty-seven, Buck was the most coveted bachelor on the island. And he didn't plan on changing that status anytime soon.

Shortly after acquiring ownership, Buck's first order of business was to make Rounds the go-to place for great entertainment. Although the establishment had welcomed many musicians over the years — filling the domed room with sounds of swing and jazz and rock — the odd circular design of the building didn't bode well for a stage.

The giant round bar in the middle, although the tavern's trademark, had always been Alvin Wilson's biggest regret because of the wasted space. The bartenders used the counter-space to mix drinks, and stored supplies underneath, which left the center of the bar virtually empty.

It was Buck who came up with the idea to build an elevated, round stage in the middle of the bar, behind the bartenders.

The bartenders still had plenty of room to work and move in the moat around the stage. And the stage itself could be visible to everyone in the room.

The finished product was even better than Buck envisioned. He dubbed his masterpiece "The Heart of Haven." All he had to do was find a great beat.

Dorothy Ann Golden was a struggling young singer in Nashville at the time. She came to Haven in the summer of '68 with her guitarist boyfriend, Sly, who had heard from a relative that an island bar was hiring seasonal entertainment.

As the story goes, Buck was instantly smitten with the petite blonde singer and her sweet southern twang. Her folksy-country sound was exactly what Buck was looking for. And Sly was a phenomenal guitarist. Buck hired them after hearing only two songs.

Dottie & Sly, as they called themselves, were a hit. Rounds Bar picked up a whole new, younger clientele, while still appealing to the gritty preferences of its regulars.

Dottie was also a talented painter and fell in love with the storybook setting of Haven. She could often be found with her easel and watercolors on the sprawling lawn of The Island Pointe Hotel at the east end of town. Dottie first gave her paintings away as free souvenirs for tourists, but soon acquiesced to their persistent donations. Buck's meager entertainment budget and the tips at Rounds only went so far.

The Pointe capitalized on her talent and appeal and began selling Dottie's works in the hotel gift shop. By September, as Haven's lush landscape exploded with bursts of color — golden yellows, burning oranges, blazing reds — Dottie had found a kindred spirit in the island itself and was heartbroken to leave.

Sly, on the other hand, was itching to get back to the glitz and glam of Nashville after using his downtime to pen a collection of original songs. He was hoping to revive rockabilly, which had lost its appeal after the death of Buddy Holly and the rising popularity of Motown. Sly's new style was less appealing to Dottie than the classic country and folksy groove of her roots, but she had always trusted his business sense.

Buck Kessner, who had been careful to hide his affections for Dottie, out of professionalism and respect, offered the duo a secure spot and pay increase for the next summer. But Sly wouldn't commit.

On the night before they were to leave, Dottie & Sly performed at their own going away party. It was a raucous celebration of locals and late-season tourists that lasted well-past closing time. And Buck, in a rare show of recklessness (he had long before learned that someone needed to stay sober at the bar), tipped back at least a dozen shots. Liquid courage.

Sly, the brooding, mysterious type, hadn't made nearly as many friends in town as his bubbly counterpart, and rarely saw any appeal in socializing after their gigs. Even on their last night, he used their "long drive home in the morning" as an excuse to bow out before the party ended. He had been storing his car on the mainland and wanted to make the 12+ hour trek to Nashville in one day.

Dottie was the last guest at the bar. Hugging and kissing everyone on their way out, she promised to stay in touch. But never gave them a concrete answer as to when, or if, she would be back.

Finally, at 4 a.m., with no more glasses to clean or floor to sweep, Dottie ran out of reasons to stay at Rounds any longer.

When she was in the back, putting away the cleaning supplies and grabbing her sweater, Buck slipped a dime in the jukebox.

"I Fall to Pieces" by Patsy Cline echoed through the emptiness as Dottie walked back into the barroom. And Buck held out his hand, inviting her to dance.

*I fall to pieces...*
*Each time I see you again.*
*I fall to pieces...*
*How can I be just your friend?*

As Buck held Dottie in his arms for the first time ever, and they swayed to the soulful lyrics, he could hardly bring himself to look at her.

He couldn't say good-bye to the 5'3" firecracker who had burst into his life just four months before, with her bright, sparkling voice and bold, vivacious spirit.

And when he did finally look down into the tear-filled eyes of the woman he knew he loved, Buck could only say one word.

"Stay."

And Dottie did.

THEIR FORTY-SEVEN-YEAR love story was nearly as legendary as the bar itself. Buck and Dottie were the sweethearts of the town. Buck with his flannel and sarcasm, Dottie all spunk and style.

She continued to pack the house whenever she sang at Rounds. On her off nights, she could be found shaking a mean martini behind the bar or commandeering the kitchen to fry up Buck's big catch of the morning. After a few years, she opened a small gallery on Pine, the street behind Main, to sell her paintings and the work of local artists.

Buck took a stab at politics for a while as Haven's mayor. But he didn't have the patience for the slow decision-making processes or petty complaints. Behind the scenes, he often turned to Dottie for diplomatic solutions. As the daughter of a Tennessee judge, she had a skill for seeing problems from an objective point-of-view. Her suggestions were logical and sound and pleased the majority much more so than Buck's.

Buck told the residents as much when he decided to step down as mayor and suggested his wife take over. Dottie adored this little town, and the locals were equally enamored by her candid authenticity. But she would only take office by means of an official vote.

She campaigned, ran, and won, uncontended. Then won the election after that. And the one after that. Dottie held office for over a decade until Buck's first bout with cancer. Then she turned over the reins to Ruby Irish, the editor of the town paper and a promising novelist.

In an odd coincidence to the Wilsons' fate, Buck and Dottie never could have children of their own. But Buck saw a bit of himself in Ruby's son, Kade, whom he'd hired as a dishwasher at age twelve. Kade's confidence, charisma, and maturity well beyond his years made him a natural for the business.

Even after he went to college, Kade always had a job at Rounds waiting for him on school breaks. He easily worked his way up to management over the summer help. When Kade moved to New York to pursue his music career, he and Buck still stayed in touch.

And in the end, when Buck — the *true* heart of Haven — was broken and brittle with cancer, he made Kade a request he couldn't refuse.

And Buck sold Rounds Bar to Kade Irish for a song.

DOTTIE REMAINED ON the island full-time even after Buck died. It was her home. And the Haveners were her family.

Her gallery, online art store, and Buck's wise investments over the years, still provide her a comfortable living. Although, she doesn't need much. Dottie always says she's been lucky to have two great loves in her life: Benjamin Eugene Kessner and Haven-on-the-Lake.

But now, at age 76, Dottie is in the fatal risk category of the horrific virus attacking the world. She knows this was one of Ruby's biggest concerns when she told Dottie the news the week before.

Ruby has always thought of Dottie as a wise mentor and dear friend, and often comes to her for advice. But Ruby doesn't need mentoring. She is one of the strongest, smartest women Dottie has ever known.

Ruby fought like hell with the government to keep their island safe, but people were now coming. They would eventually bring the virus. It was only a matter of time.

And Dottie Kessner needs to stand by her friend.

# HAVEN

SATURDAY, APRIL 1
9:00 A.M.

ON THE MORNING OF THE emergency Town Hall meeting, Frank and Dottie are already sitting outside Rounds Bar when Ruby and her husband, Jack, arrive.

Jack's father, Frank, must have been first. He's sitting in a folding chair by the door holding a white Styrofoam cup, which is steaming. Dottie is next to him, in a matching chair, also holding a steaming cup, with leopard-print gloves. Ruby notices a giant thermos at Dottie's feet. She brought coffee for everyone. Of course she did.

April is unpredictable on Haven. Some years, there is still several feet of snow on the ground and everyone is coasting around town on snowmobiles, since the island doesn't allow cars. Hockey is played on Main Street every Sunday. And the downtown area looks like a scene out of a Dickens classic...or a Hallmark movie.

Other years, like this one, there is barely any snow at all, and the weather is already above freezing, with some days in the mid-forties. This is when golf cart heaters are running at full tilt, and the clear plastic flaps are pulled down to shield riders from the wind. It's not nearly as appealing to tool around town, and there's no weekly hockey game, so residents see each other less.

The meeting today will be the first time the residents have all been together since the annual New Year's Eve party.

Because Haven-on-the-Lake was closed to non-residents in November, and no one was exposed to the virus, Ruby took it upon herself to disregard the mainland's shelter-in-place regulations. Or, moreover, she deemed Haven one unified "place" where they could all shelter together.

Ruby has avoided any large gatherings herself and prohibited them from being posted on social media, but that's the only new rule she imposed. Because of their isolation, there's no need for face masks or social distancing or the closing of any businesses. It's been life as usual for Haveners. Until now.

"It's freezing out here, why aren't you inside?" Ruby asks the senior duo as she steps out of the golf cart's passenger side and pulls out a large white box from the seat between her and Jack. "Isn't Kade here yet?"

"Oh, he is," Frank answers, meeting her at the curb to take the box from her hands. "But you don't need us all up in your business when you tell the kids. You go on in, we're fine out here until you're ready."

Dottie nods her head and smiles. She's in full make-up and her white-blonde curls are peeking out from beneath a black fur hat. The air smells of bitter coffee and Chanel N°5.

"We're fine, dear," Dottie says. "Don't worry about us."

"Of course, I'm worried about you," Ruby says, unfastening another box from the rear seat of the cart. "It's my job to worry about you."

She sets down the box on the steps and bangs on the door, then gestures through the glass for Kade to open. He's pulling stools off tables that were uprooted the night before for cleaning.

Ruby imagines Rounds was Friday-night-full, as usual, since it's the only bar open in the winter besides Charlie's. Rounds is for music and a party. Charlie's is for poker...and a party. Jack is usually at Charlie's, but last night he was home with Ruby.

"Sorry, Mom," Kade says after unlocking and opening the door, only just then noticing his grandpa and Dottie. "Oh jeez, I didn't see you guys out here!"

Ruby stands back and waves the two in.

"Kade, do you have coffee on?" She asks, setting the bulky box on the bar.

"I was just getting to that," he says, pulling down more stools. "Had to turn up the heat, set down all the chairs, you know..."

"Oh, I have plenty for y'all," Dottie says, holding up the thermos with one hand and a floral canvas bag with the other. "And still-warm banana bread, too. But I'll put on a fresh pot as well. If that's okay with you, Kade?"

After owning Rounds for more than forty years, Dottie still knows her way around like it's home. But she never over-steps her boundaries.

"Please, Dottie," Kade says. "Thank you."

Before Frank lays his coat over a bar stool to claim his spot, he clarifies the best vantage point.

"Rubes, you gonna be on the stage?"

"I'll have to be," she says. "If everyone shows up, this bar will just about be at maximum capacity. I don't want to have to yell."

She looks to her son. "Kade, we'll need extra microphones, in case people have questions."

"In case?" Frank chuckles as he heads out to gather his folding chairs. "Oh. They'll have questions."

"I did prepare informational packets for everyone," Ruby says while unwrapping the thick, green scarf from around her neck and taking off her down-filled jacket.

"But I do not want anyone to see them before I make the initial announcement. Otherwise, it'll be a flurry of paper-rustling chaos. Kade, can you put these boxes behind the bar? And please send everyone back to the office when they get here."

THE REST OF THE IRISH family arrives in order of age, oldest to youngest — Paul, then Georgia, then Declan.

The siblings had sent a flurry of responses to their mother's morning text, but their dad had simply responded on her behalf: No need to panic. See you at 10 sharp!

Once Declan arrives at 10:15, Ruby fills them in on the government's plan: that Haven-on-the-Lake has been selected as Immunity Community #1.

She gives them each a packet, which is filled with answers to the many questions she asked the "experts" so far. But her kids want verbal answers instead, which Ruby knows will be the case at the Town Hall Meeting as well.

It's going to be a very long day.

"How long have you known about this, Mom?" Georgia asks.

"A couple weeks now," Ruby says. "I couldn't tell you, for obvious reasons. It was completely confidential. And I didn't want to worry you…in case it didn't happen. And, believe me, I tried very hard to make this *not* happen. It was only just officially confirmed, on record, this morning."

"On your call with the Vice President?" Kade asks.

"*Of the United States?*" Declan asks.

"No. Of the PTA." Kade shoots a smile at his mom.

She rolls her eyes and nods at Declan.

"Did Paul know about all this?" Kade asks, his tone inquisitive, not jealous. He knows his older brother is an obsessive genius and was following the virus since early November, before Kade had even heard of it. He looks at Paul.

"You're like our own personal Gossi," Kade says, referring to the brilliant, unflappable CDC Director who has been the sweetheart of the national news.

"Yes," Ruby says. "I brought Paul in last week to help me ask educated questions to Mr. Gossi."

"Wait. You talked to him? Stephen Gossi?" Georgia is even more impressed with that than the call with the V.P. Again, everyone's kind of crushing on Gossi.

"Oh, honey, you wouldn't believe how many people I've talked to," Ruby says, taking off her reading glasses to rub her eyes. She hasn't had a full night sleep in weeks. "Frankly, it's been overwhelming. But now, it is what it is. And we need to make the best of it."

Ruby is sitting at Kade's desk which faces the door of his small office. Paul is in the only other chair, pulled up to the desk, with his back to his siblings. He's already massacring the informational handout with a red pen. Georgia and Kade are both leaning against the wall on either side of the door. Declan, the tallest of the bunch, has made the top of the filing cabinet his own personal breakfast bar of coffee, orange juice, bottled water, and a slice of Dottie's bread. Jack has just come into view with fresh coffee for Ruby.

"What's wrong?" he asks of his uncharacteristically silent family. "I mean, besides the obvious."

"Nothing," Ruby says, taking the glass from Jack and thanking him. The mug bears the Rounds Bar logo on one side and *THERE MAY OR MAY NOT BE ALCOHOL IN HERE* on the other. That, and the smell of hazelnut creamer that Jack must have added, makes her smile a bit. Normalcy, peace, humor. She hasn't felt any of that in a while.

"I'm just realizing it's the first time we've all been in the same room since I got the news," Ruby says. "And, well, I feel bad that I couldn't tell you sooner. But, I'm just so thankful we're all together right now."

She sips and goes on, resuming managerial mode.

"There are going to be a lot of questions of all of you after today. Because people will assume you're in the know. I suggest your canned answer be that you aren't privy to any more information than anyone else. And then, suggest that they send me an email. Paul has set up a specific email address just for this. It's on the handout. He'll be spearheading the response team."

Paul looks up from his paper and nods, then resumes writing, reading, and writing some more.

"Each one of you has strengths and talents that will be put to good use in the next few months," she continues. "Georgia, you're about to expand your fashion portfolio. The ballrooms of both The Majestic and The Pointe will now become production centers for masks and gowns. It's all-hands-on-deck to supply the hospitals with PPE, personal protective equipment. The gowns are a simple pattern. Practically no-sew. The supplies will be arriving next week."

Ruby sips her coffee again and continues.

"Going forward, most states will be requiring citizens to wear masks in public buildings. But disposable surgical masks should be reserved for health care professionals. So we'll be making washable fabric masks to keep up with public demand. You'll have plenty of help with these projects, but you'll be a key player. Okay?"

Georgia nods; her auburn messy bun adding spunk to her seriousness. At nearly forty, Georgia could pass for a decade younger.

"Declan," Ruby looks at her youngest son. "Each arriving family will be provided with a golf cart for transportation until the weather warms. Then bikes will be the primary mode, as usual. I will need you to combine your inventory with Paul's, and all the other available vehicles on the island. They'll need to be safety-checked, tuned up, repaired, you know the drill. You'll have a full staff for this, too. And, don't worry, you'll be fully compensated. But we'll discuss those numbers later."

Declan salutes as he browses the info packet.

"Kade," she turns toward her second-youngest. "Rounds will be open as usual, with high-season hours. Entertainment is actually encouraged — for a feeling of normalcy and stress relief, per the team psychologist, Aditi Ahmed. You'll all get to know her well. She seems great. Charlie's will be open, too. All the other owners of key businesses are being contacted to see if they meet the qualifications to come. If they didn't have the illness, or don't pass an antibody test, they will not be allowed in the first wave. Their businesses will be outsourced."

"First wave?" Georgia asks.

"Of Survivors," Paul says, looking up from his edits to nod at the paper in Georgia's hand. "It's in the packet."

"This will all be covered today," Ruby says. "But, yes, right now, the plan is for Survivors…that's what we're calling them for lack of a better word…to arrive in three waves. The first will be those required to open essential businesses and start the gown, mask, and sanitizer operations."

"Sanitizer?" Three of the Irish siblings ask in unison. Paul looks up, audibly sighs, and then resumes writing. No doubt, he's silently grumbling about why he bothered to type up the information at all.

"The old distillery will now be making hand sanitizer," Ruby says. "Hundreds of unemployed people will now have jobs; income they wouldn't have otherwise been bringing in. That's part of the appeal of coming here. Well, that, and the fact that they get to live with no restrictions. Haven will truly be their haven."

"Good for future business," Paul says, without looking up. "Better than TripAdvisor."

What Paul lacks in showing emotion, his brothers always say, he makes up for in being annoying.

"No restrictions at all?" Georgia asks. "Not even social distancing? Is that safe? Are we sure they're no longer contagious? What about high-risk residents…like Dottie? And Grandpa?"

Ruby knows Georgia is also thinking of her children, one of whom has asthma, and her husband, Alek, who has been diabetic since childhood. It pains Ruby to see her daughter's fear. Georgia's family has been Ruby's deepest concern.

"Again, this will all be covered at the meeting," Ruby says. "But those arriving will all have tested negative for the illness. And they will have been tested for antibodies as well. Unfortunately, since this is all happening so fast, neither test is a hundred percent foolproof. And there are other concerns as well."

"Secondary infections," Paul says. "And virus mutations."

Ruby nods, slow and heavy with the weight of her worries.

"This will be the most difficult news I deliver today," Ruby says. "That, yes, there is a possibility of contagion. But the *hope* is that the Unexposed…that's what Haveners are being called…the Unexposed. The hope is that we will not catch the virus from the Survivors."

"Hope?" Kade asks. "This is all based on hope?"

"It has to be, Son," Ruby says. "Even if we weren't facing this now, we would be someday. And, honestly, this is the most protection we could ask for. The best-case scenario, really."

"Besides not opening at all," Declan says. "Until there's a vaccine."

"That's no longer an option, honey," Ruby says. "Believe me, I tried."

Declan nods once, knowing damn well his mother would have tried. Knowing she's feeling defeated right now. And knowing when to shut up.

"At least for this summer, we'll be able to control who comes to Haven," Ruby says. "That's better than most cities, and countries, can do."

Ruby looks at the clock above the door; its red numbers glow 10:50 a.m. under a Coors Lite mountain scene.

"It's almost eleven now," she says. "I'd like the Town Hall to begin at 2:00. If I send a text right now, that'll give people three hours. But you know some will be here by noon, so we need to start getting things ready. Do you have any more questions for me before we get rolling?"

"Only about a thousand," Georgia attempts a smile. "But they can wait."

"I'm good," Kade says, waving the packet.

"Same," Declan says. "I'm sure you and Einstein over here [he nods toward Paul] answered about a hundred more than I'd even know to ask."

"Okay," Ruby says. "I'm going to need some time alone to prep. Dottie said she'll take care of getting people fed. I'm sure she'll have a full-blown potluck coordinated in twenty minutes. Can you make sure everyone has whatever else they need – drinks, napkins, whatever?"

"On it, Cap'n," Kade moves to head out the door, but her ever-responsible son turns around and offers a wink of reassurance to his mother. "You'll do great, Mom."

He clamps his dad on the shoulder on the way out and the two exchange the smile and nod of two men trusting each other.

"Thanks, sweetie." She smiles after him and then at her daughter.

"Georgia, honey, I already contacted Chuck Brown and told him to plan to open the theatre today." She's referring to The Comet, Haven's vintage movie theatre on Main Street, a few doors down from Rounds. "Told him I'd give him the details this morning. Can you handle that? He can run movies for the kids while their parents attend the meeting. I'm sure you can get Kara and Macy to help coordinate that."

"Sure, Mom." Georgia looks as if she wants to say something else, but doesn't. She kisses her dad's cheek on the way out the door, but avoids his eyes. Ruby knows Georgia is dreading the call she has to make now to Alek, who has thanked his mother-in-law more than once for keeping his family safe. She feels another wave of worry for the children of their town.

"Deck, can you handle the sound system, please?" Ruby says to Declan as he gathers his breakfast mess. "As I told Kade, we'll need mics set up for questions."

"No problem," he says, tossing his trash ball into the garbage can across the room like a basketball shot. "I gotchu, Mom."

He fist-bumps his dad on the way out and says, "We got this."

They can always rely on Declan to make light of things.

Paul continues to jot notes on the handout. He's likely been up all night finding more thorough answers to any follow-up questions.

"Any news on Mia?" Ruby asks Paul. She's referring to Mia Holm, Georgia's college roommate and the silent partner in Georgia's boho-chic island boutique, *Bohavia*. Since Mia is technically a business owner, and caught the virus on a Christmas trip to Italy, there's a chance she could qualify for the Community. As a fashion designer, Mia could help with the mask or gown operations, which is a point in her favor to make the Survivors list. But Ruby doesn't want to get Georgia's hopes up until she knows for sure.

"Yes, she forwarded me her test results last night and she's in the clear," Paul says. "Now she needs government clearance."

The government's Immunity Community Task Force is doing extensive background checks on all of Ruby's recommended business owners. Even if they qualify medically, they can't have so much as a minor infraction on their record. A peaceful, cohesive community is imperative for all involved.

"Okay, let me know as soon as you know," Ruby says. "I'm worried about Georgia and would love to give her something positive to look forward to in this mess. Anyway, I need a little time to prep, can you give me a few minutes alone, hon?"

Paul has already resumed writing, but nods at his mom and dad and gathers his things to hustle out.

Jack shuts the door and moves into the room and around the desk to be closer to his wife. Uniting under pressure has always been a strength of theirs, and Ruby considers Jack to be the true rock of their family.

Jack is one of those lucky guys whose boyish cuteness lingered well into his twenties, and then transformed into a distinguished sexy. He's never given much thought to his looks, which makes him even more handsome. His dark hair now has just enough grey, his dimples have deepened, and his eye-crinkling smile is a sweet, familiar comfort to Ruby.

"You did good, love," he says, turning her chair toward him so he can kiss her on the lips. "And we've got some great kids there."

"That, we do," Ruby says. "They handled it well."

Ruby leans her head against the office chair, and sighs.

"I'm just so sad for Georgia," she says. "Being a mother takes this to a whole new level. I'm worried about her. I'm worried about everyone. It makes me feel so...*helpless*...that one sick person could change everything we have here."

"I know," Jack says. "But we have to have faith that they won't. That we'll survive this and make it through. We've been lucky to avoid it as long as we have. Thanks to you. And we *will* make it through."

"Keep that attitude, please," Ruby says, attempting a smile. "Promise? No matter what."

"I promise," Jack says. "I'd promise you anything, darlin'. You know that. Now do you need anything else before the meeting?"

"A cure?" Ruby says. "Vaccine? A time machine!"

"Would if I could, my dear. All three." Jack kisses her lips, nose, and forehead as he's done a million times since they met as twenty-somethings almost forty years ago. "We really do 'got this,' Mrs. Mayor. I promise we do."

"I hope so," Ruby says.

But she really does wish she had a time machine.

# FRANK

Francesco Guiseppe Irish is first-generation American, born of Guiseppe and Emma Irish, who met and married in New York City when Emma was eighteen and Guiseppe was a decade older. They had three children in rapid succession, a boy and two girls.

Frankie knew early on, after being teased by his neighborhood friends, that there was no way *Irish* was his family's real name. Rumors came and went that a run from the law was involved. But this was never confirmed by his father, who would simply say, while lifting his beer: "We're Irishmen in America now and that is all that matters."

It was a questionable "accident" that landed his father (and his car) in a lake and left Emma a widow at thirty-four. Frank, at only fifteen, felt obligated to take care of his mother and sisters.

He took odd jobs as a hardware store stock boy, mechanic's assistant, and handyman. Then was hired by his best friend's dad to work in their family's construction business, Costello & Sons Construction.

A few years later, when Frank caught his sister, Caroline, sneaking around with one of the Costello sons, Lorenzo, he gave the kid a broken nose. And nearly lost his job. But Lorenzo proved his good intentions by proposing to Caroline within the year. And Frank was comforted to know that his sister would be well provided for.

By twenty-one, Frank had saved enough money to move out on his own. His mother was remarried by then, to George Buscemi, the stout, hairy owner of their corner deli. And Frank's youngest sister, Lucy, was the first in their family to go to college.

Frank, a handsome young man with his father's (unconfirmed) Italian traits, had half-heartedly dated over the years, but only to bide his time while waiting for Iris Bianchi.

Iris Bianchi, his youngest sister's best friend who grew up next door, had harbored a crush on Frank most of her life. And she made no secret of it.

"Iris says she's gonna marry you someday," Lucy told him, more than once. "She thinks you're the most handsome man in the world and that she's the Scarlett O'Hara to your Rhett Butler."

Frank would pretend to ignore his sister's nonsense, but the truth was, he thought Iris was the prettiest girl he'd ever seen up close. She did resemble Scarlett O'Hara with her dark hair, light eyes, and airy charm. But Frank refused to ask her out until she graduated high school.

Iris beat him to it.

"You gonna move away without ever even asking me out, Frank Irish?" She said from her porch swing as he loaded his few belongings into a Costello & Sons pick-up truck the day he moved to his own apartment.

"I'm only moving two streets away," he hollered back. "I'll be back on Sunday for dinner."

"Okay," Iris smiled. "I'll be ready at 7:00. You can take me to a movie after you eat."

"Oh, I can, can I?" Frank said as he meandered over to her tiny patch of lawn.

"Yep," Iris said, standing up to head into her house. "You're a lucky man, Mr. Irish, that I am a very patient woman."

The wooden screen door slammed shut behind her, leaving Frank alone on the grass with the goofy grin of a man in love.

Frank proposed to Iris on her twentieth birthday and they had a small wedding in the backyard of the Costello's vacation home in upstate New York.

When the pastor pronounced them husband and wife, and presented the couple to the small crowd, Iris proudly declared that she was now *Iris Irish!* And everyone had laughed. She tossed her bouquet to her maid-of-honor, Lucy, who was engaged to her college boyfriend. And then cued the catering staff to serve champagne to the guests right then and there.

Because that's just the kind of woman Iris was — happy to make people happy, and proud of the man she loved.

They honeymooned at The Island Pointe Hotel, Haven-on-the-Lake, and Iris made Frank promise they would return every summer with the brood of kids she hoped "to start popping out right away!"

But things didn't quite go as planned.

Frank, not being a Costello son, had gone as far as he could in the business as a foreman with a modest salary. And Iris struggled to get pregnant for over a year.

When Frank was offered a position that could lead to partnership at a construction company in Lakewood, Ohio, they both thought a change of scenery would do them good. Iris, always up for new adventures, embraced the move with refreshed hope as they loaded a trailer behind their turquoise Chevy Bel Air and waved good-bye to New York.

She found out she was pregnant within a month. And Jonathan Francesco Irish (Jack for short), was born on the first day of spring.

The pregnancy had been easy, and the delivery smooth, and Iris had hoped to give Jack a sibling right away. Iris was an only child and had always envied how close in age Frank and his sisters were. But Iris only suffered miscarriages. One after another, for several years.

There was no known medical reason, at first, for why Iris couldn't conceive. And it dimmed her sparkle at times. But she always rallied for Jack and Frank because she relished being a mom and a wife.

Frank did become partner in the company and worked long hours, including weekends. But Iris had made good friends in Ohio and was content with their life there. She volunteered at the school, became a master in the kitchen, and loved watching her "two favorite men" shoot hoops on their Sundays at home.

Iris was only thirty years old when she was diagnosed with ovarian cancer.

It had already spread to her lymph nodes by the time they found it, and her odds for survival were slim. While that same diagnosis today would likely have a better result, Iris lost the brutal battle in only seven months.

Jack was nine. And Frank Irish was lost without his wife.

He struggled as a single father, working six days a week building houses, and often relying on the kindness of neighbors to look after Jack. Because he had been so busy with the business before Iris's death, Frank's only real bond with his son was basketball once in a while. Without Iris as their glue, the two just drifted apart.

Jack had inherited Frank's mechanical skills, but he was much more into technology — always taking apart radios, toasters, blenders, or whatever small appliances people left at their curbs. Frank spent his only day off watching sports, with a beer, then Scotch, in his hand. The two were rarely together in the same room for more than a hot dog dinner.

When Iris had been alive, the one vacation they took every year (besides road trips back to New York) was a four-day summer weekend to Haven-on-the-Lake. Iris would put spare cash in a jar labeled **Haven FUNd** all year long. And the look on her face as they ferried to the island was worth every dollar they scrimped and saved.

Iris always insisted they sit in the open-air seats on top so they could "jump-start their summer glow." Then she would alternate tilting her face to the sun and using binoculars to scout out the shore. Jack reflected the joy of his mother and shared her love for Haven, especially Island Pointe where he could run on the spacious lawn.

Iris would pack a picnic lunch for their first afternoon every year and sit in one of the white Adirondack chairs that speckled the hotel's massive grounds, saying how "perfectly happy" she was.

They would rent bikes the second day, with a pull-behind trailer for Jack, until he could handle the trip on a two-wheel bike of his own. It was typically a two-hour tour to bike the eight miles around the island, but Iris insisted they take their time and choose dream homes along the way. Frank would point out the details that marked certain eras and trends, and Iris would quiz him on dates before she checked the historical signs. Frank could usually guess their construction within a year or two.

While Frank preferred the grand designs of Victorian-style mansions, Iris said she just wanted a cottage with a white picket fence and a garden.

She was too sick to go to Haven the summer before she died, but asked that her ashes be spread there "in a garden that soaked up the sun."

Frank's grief for Iris was dark and Ohio winters were long. As the years went on, he spent most of his nights with a bottle, while his son holed up in his room. He would drive Jack to New York to drop him off with his mother and sisters for summers and holidays, but then use work as an excuse to rush back to Ohio himself.

Frank's family worried that he was following in his father's booze-soaked footsteps. But Jack never outed his father. He would simply shrug when asked about his dad and then go off to play with his cousins...or take apart a radio.

The year Jack turned twelve, Frank said he was too busy to drive to New York over Christmas. He told his mother that Jack was old enough to take care of himself, so he didn't need anyone to come and babysit during school break. But Frank's mom and sisters weren't buying it.

The three women drove all night in Caroline's station wagon, with gifts and food and cleaning supplies, to show up at Frank's door on December 27$^{th}$.

When they found a disastrous bachelor pad and a trash bin full of empty liquor bottles, their worries were confirmed.

Frank's mother, Emma, vowed she wasn't going to let alcohol destroy another person she loved. She sent her daughters home and stayed in Ohio to care for Jack, and force Frank into detox. It was brutal and ugly and messy. And the sweaty, shaky, moody withdrawals were nearly impossible to handle at times, but Emma was determined to save her son.

The first time Frank admitted he had a problem out loud was at an AA meeting down at the Y. His sponsor, Rich Patterson, became a Godsend to the family and helped them all navigate their way through recovery.

Emma discovered that Iris had left a helpful circle of close friends and was well-respected at the school. The counselor found a therapist for Jack to help him work through the loss of his mother and distrustful fear of his dad. Frank eventually joined some therapy sessions as well.

By the time Emma went back to New York in early February, her son was forty days sober, with a solid support system. And he was committed to earning Jack's trust by becoming a man he could respect. Jack, who would be thirteen soon, was growing into a bright young man with his mother's compassionate heart.

When school was dismissed in June, Frank suggested they resume their annual tradition to Haven-on-the-Lake and fulfill Iris's wishes to spread her ashes there. Frank extended their reservations to an entire week so they could take their time to find "the perfect garden in the sun" for Iris to be laid to rest.

The first day at Island Pointe was heartbreaking and awkward and quiet. And the bike ride around the island was full of ghosts instead of dreams.

Frank feared it might have been a mistake to extend the trip, but he saw something light up in his boy when they chartered a fishing trip.

It was a perfect day on the lake, 80 and sunny with water like glass. Jack beamed when he reeled in a Rainbow Trout, laughed when he caught a Chinook Salmon, and cheered out loud when he snagged a giant Northern Pike.

Sipping cold orange sodas and smelling of summertime as they coasted back to shore, Frank felt a wave of love for his son that finally outshined his grief.

"I can see why Mom wanted to stay here forever," Jack said, his dark hair windblown and cheeks shining pink. "It's my favorite place in the world so far."

Frank agreed with his son, and didn't want the week to end.

Frank asked Captain Joe Chapman, as he fileted fish on the dock at the end of the day, if Haven had a hardware store. He hadn't seen one in town; hadn't seen many practical businesses, really.

Captain Joe said there was only a hardware section in the back of the General Store, on Center Street in Centerhaven, where most of the locals lived. Otherwise, any hardware needs required a trip to the mainland Ace.

Frank and Jack rented bikes again for their fourth day on the island and decided to do a little searching for this mysterious Centerhaven. In all their years of coming to the island, they had never even heard of this tiny sub-city. And they soon discovered why.

The ferries to Haven-on-the-Lake only accessed the island by two docks, both on the south side of the town. These docks filtered passengers directly on to Main Street, where the ninety percent of the businesses and restaurants stood. Pine Street, just behind Main, was only just starting to fill with more shops. But Main Street was the hot spot of Haven and tourists spent most of their time there.

Rounds Bar had prime real estate in the center of town, and was flanked in both directions by a variety of awning-covered gift shops, bakeries, fudgeries, boutique hotels, a small movie theatre, bike rentals (later, they'd add golf carts), and more restaurants and bars. All impeccably maintained and freshly painted in cool, calm, coastal colors of white, pink, yellow, turquoise, and mint.

As each end of Main Street curved northward, the businesses give way to residential zoning, horse stables, the two big hotels — The Majestic to the west and Island Pointe to the east — and then more horse stables. Cars weren't allowed on Haven (except for one ambulance), and horses and carriages were the primary modes of transportation, besides bikes.

Main Street stretched around the circumference of the island to form the infamous 8-Mile Loop that Frank, Iris and Jack would bike every year, along with every other tourist on the island. But beyond the two big hotels, there wasn't much to see besides private houses, rocky beaches, and paths to the inland woods.

On the north side of the island, there was one small taco stand called Cabanas, which was like an oasis in the desert.

Once you got there, it was still another hour ride back to Main Street (no one rode fast on Haven) and there were no other restaurants until town. Or so Jack and Frank had always thought.

For years, they assumed there was no other choice than to keep going around the island with the rest of the herd. But Captain Joe informed them otherwise. Turns out, there were several cut-through streets…that led to another downtown!

That day, Frank and Jack left The Pointe, traveling northeast as usual, but instead of biking The Loop, they turned inland on the first street they saw, Fairway Drive, which they hadn't noticed before.

There were a few small cottages on the narrow road and then nothing until the Haven Island Golf Course (also a new discovery). And then more of nothing…except cemeteries. Three different cemeteries in a row, which Jack found creepy, but interesting.

Why weren't all Haveners buried in one? Were they enemy families of Haven past? How many more cemeteries were there on the island? He asked his dad if they could get a few Haven-on-the-Lake history books once they returned to town. This little island obviously had stories to tell.

After another ten minutes or so, Frank and Jack started seeing signs of life. Completely different than that of fairytale-perfect Main Street.

A series of residential streets stemmed off Fairway, and the landscape didn't look much different than a modest suburban Ohio neighborhood. They turned onto Heritage Drive. It was long enough for about a dozen small, neat, plain homes — mostly ranches — with sidewalks, driveways, and generous yards between them. One street connected to another until they found themselves on Center Street, where the only businesses were.

Center Street was a much, much less glamorous version of Main, if it could be compared at all. It consisted of a diner, a pharmacy, a barber shop, the post office, a bank, a small library, a large general store, and a couple of vacant storefronts. At the far end was a medical clinic, with a sign that boasted a larger building to be coming the year before, but there wasn't even a hint of construction yet. Beyond that was only the school: one building between two parking lots, that doubled as basketball courts, and a soccer field in back, surrounded by a running track.

Center Street abruptly ended at Haven-on-the-Lake State Park.

They turned around and parked their bikes at Maxwell's General Store and headed inside.

"General" was about as accurate as a description could be. Half of the twenty-plus aisles were filled with groceries, while the others stocked clothing, sporting goods, toys, home décor, small appliances, medical supplies, you name it. And, as Captain Joe had said, there was a hardware section in the back, which opened to an outside lawn and garden center. The whole place smelled like a combination of fried chicken, fertilizer, and floral air freshener.

There was a deli and ice cream counter near the entrance, advertising hand-dipped cones, which had caught Jack's eye on the way in. A teenage girl was sitting behind the counter, watching a black-and-white television with rabbit ears. She served Frank and Jack each a heaping double-scoop of Blue Moon on a sugar cone, a mutual favorite of theirs.

When they took a seat on the bench out front, Frank struck up a conversation with an older gentleman enjoying a cone himself. He asked about the two abandoned stores and what they used to be.

"Oh, I remember that one best as Hank's Bar," the man said, pointing to the store directly across. "Lost plenty a poker game there. And then Hank's daughter, Suzy, turned it into a bakery and flower shop for a while. But she passed. Lung cancer. And it's been empty for quite some time now."

"And the other one, at the end of the street?" Frank asked.

"That there was Hanson's Market, Centerhaven's main store before the General here took over," he said, jutting a thumb toward the building behind them.

"This used to be the Elk's Lodge," he said. "Home of dinner dances, fish fries, and crusty old guys telling war stories. But when The Island Pointe moved in, to compete with Madge, the construction families took over Centerhaven and needed more than Hanson's could offer. Them builders' wives just kept poppin' out babies who needed…oh, you know…*everything*. So, the Elks sold to the Maxwells who opened up the General. They were already making a killing with fudge, but…well…greedy, I guess."

"What happened to Hanson's?" Frank asked.

"Tried to compete," the man said. "But just couldn't. Closed their doors 'bout a year after. And started making fudge!"

He laughed and shook his head.

"Ooh, if I had a nickel every time a Hanson-Maxwell fight broke out at a bar!"

"I knew it!" Jack said, his ice cream now making a blue puddle at his feet. "Is that why there are so many separate cemeteries? Were there island rivals?"

"Son, there are a lot more interesting Haven stories than the Hansons and Maxwells," the man said. "The construction of Madge could fill a few history books itself. What a clusterwhack. But, yes, I imagine there's a reason why some families refused to bury their dead with the likes of others."

"Think old Hanson's Market is still pretty solid?" Frank asked.

"Hell, yeah," the man said. "All the buildings in Centerhaven are sturdy bastards. It's the ones down on Main Street I wouldn't trust. Them things can't last a season without somebody fixin' somethin.'"

Frank finished his cone and wiped his mouth with his hand. He had given all his napkins to Jack who was a sticky blue mess.

"Thanks for your information, sir," Frank said. "I'd like to go take a peek at Hanson's. Think anyone would mind?"

"Not a bit," the man said.

"Great. Thanks for your help," Frank said, extending his hand. "I'm Frank, by the way. Frank Irish. And this is my son, Jack."

"Herbert," the man said, with a grip that defied his age. "Herbert Hanson."

Jack's eyes flew wide, recognizing the name, and Herb couldn't help but smirk.

He offered to give the duo a personal tour of his family's old grocery store. Frank was impressed by the strong, quality structure, still well-intact. Some updated electrical work and a few reinforcements would be needed to bring it up to code. And, of course, it needed a facelift, but that was nothing Frank couldn't handle himself.

When Jack went back to The General to wash up, Frank had a talk with Herb Hanson.

"WHAT WOULD YOU THINK if we lived here?" Frank asked Jack at dinner that night. "I mean full-time, all year-round?"

Jack, who had been devouring his pepperoni hand-tossed at Slice of Haven, looked up with a sunburned nose and his mother's hopeful expression. He bore an uncanny resemblance to Iris, with his dark hair, light eyes, and deep dimples. And his smile had a way of illuminating his whole face, just like his mother's did.

As Frank went on to detail his idea of opening a hardware store and building repair service, he saw Jack's boyish energy return for the first time since Iris had passed. That night, her "two favorite guys" started to plan their future together. They decided not to spread Iris's ashes until Haven was officially their home. And by the end of the summer, it was.

At first, their budget was tight, so Frank built an apartment above the store where he and Jack would live for a few years. But Frank always kept his eye out for a deal on a decent cottage, where he could build a wooden fence and add a little garden.

When they found just that three years later, Frank and Jack spent a September afternoon planting iris bulbs along the fence in the sunniest part of the yard. That's where they spread Iris's ashes. The pink, yellow, and orange array of flowers bloomed like a sunrise the following spring, which got bigger and brighter every year.

Jack was a clever, helpful, mild-mannered boy who didn't complain about working at the store. But Frank could tell it wasn't his passion, so he only used his son on an as-needed basis. Jack had made some good friends, which was an improvement from Ohio, and Frank made sure his son had plenty of time to go off and be a kid.

Jack's curiosity for how things worked made him a natural mechanic, which wasn't much use on an island where cars were not allowed. Haven was still years away from switching from horses to golf carts.

The island marina, however, was full of boats that needed repairs...and held great potential for Jack. The dockhands in the high season made hefty tips tying off and gassing up the boats of Haven's generous tourists. Frank didn't give Jack a hassle when he asked to work there a few days a week. Frank had gotten a great deal on a 37-foot Tartan sailboat when they first moved to town, which was anchored in the marina. He asked Jack to spruce it up.

Things happened fast once fellow boat owners saw Jack at work. He meticulously restored the Tartan's grey, faded teak to a thick honey sheen, which took ten years off the old girl. It was tedious, sticky work that no one wanted to do, and Jack barely had time for the requests to work his magic on others.

Over the years, he learned his way around the decks, hulls, cabins, engines, and rudders of everything from single handle sailboats to speedboats to luxury yachts. All summer long, when he wasn't helping at the store, he was near the water. He worked the dock, tinkered with the Tartan, helped with repairs...and always made time to fish.

When he got his captain's license at nineteen, Jack had the bright idea to start a business of his own, teaching tourists to sail by day and taking them for cruises at sunset. This was just the start of Jack's nautical business plans. He had dreams to expand the sailing business to several boats, and then own a fishing charter.

In the off-season, he helped his dad with building repairs around the island and worked on growing his businesses. He didn't have any plans to leave Haven and neither did his dad. Like Iris, they were "perfectly happy" there. And Frank was at peace knowing he'd made the right move.

Although, rarely did a day go by without Frank wishing his beautiful Iris Irish were alive to live her dream.

SHE WOULD BE SO PROUD of her handsome son now; a good, solid, successful man. And a great provider for his wife and kids.

Iris would adore her daughter-in-law, Ruby, because she would have seen the look on Jack's face the first day he brought her home. She would have loved how much Ruby loved Haven. And she would have seen some of herself in the woman's resilient spirit.

Even now that some stupid flu is making the world go crazy, Frank believes his Iris would remain hopeful and positive...and say everything would be okay. And he planned to do the same, by keeping the Haveners calm.

He was fine with opening the island. They needed to get back to work. And Frank Irish wasn't about to let fear take over their town.

# HAVEN

As expected, the Town Hall announcement was met with an uproar of resistance, outrage, fear...and questions, questions, questions. The meeting went on long into the night. And there were several more meetings and discussions during the days and weeks to follow.

Throughout the winter, Haveners had been preparing for their first-ever summer without tourists. And although many would struggle financially, they figured out ways to survive. They knew they would all make it through and that it was right to close their borders. As things got worse in the world, Haveners felt lucky to be spared from the disease, and grateful for Ruby's decision to isolate them so early on.

But now, as if with the rip of a band-aid, they were open, uncovered, exposed.

Not only were they told that hundreds of people would soon be moving into their town. But they were also faced with the decision to stay on the island or leave.

The government had offered to pay for the relocation of any Haven resident who did not want to be a part of the Immunity Community. Their housing costs would be covered for the summer and they would be provided a modest stipend for their living expenses.

Those who were vulnerable in health and age, or had young children to consider, were most tempted to take the offer. If even one Survivor was contagious, and the virus spread through the island, their medical center wasn't equipped to handle an influx of disease.

But once they left the island, they would be deemed Exposed, and there was no definite plan as to when they could return without putting the other Haveners at risk.

As this mental ping-pong continued — stay or go, stay or go, stay or go — there were positives to consider, too. Friends and neighbors discussed those at length over many a pint at Rounds. Frank Irish usually led the charge on why this could be a good thing.

Haveners knew they would have to open their docks sooner or later, to property owners if no one else, but controlling who came in would certainly lower the immediate risk.

Also, the island's borders would be protected, for this summer anyway, from any untested intruders, which wouldn't be possible otherwise. Mayor Irish had fought hard to confirm extra security, both water and air surveillance, and the government complied by enlisting the military and a private team.

The mayor had also asked for extra medical help, including supplies, ventilators, personal protective gear, and several healthcare workers who were familiar with the disease. And she was promised all of that, too.

Of course, the government had their own agenda to make this experiment succeed, so they agreed to the mayor's demands and gave her just about anything she asked. It helped that she made it clear that she would relay all conversations to the public through transcripts – or recordings, if requested.

Haveners knew this kind of government aid would not have been provided to their island if they hadn't been chosen for this. Haven-on-the-Lake would be neglected and ignored, like so many other small towns, if they weren't on the President's radar as his now infamous "Beacon of Hope."

So there definitely were some advantages to becoming an Immunity Community. And Haveners helped each other focus on the good.

In the end, after three sleepless weeks and hundreds of hours of discussions, all 183 full-time residents of Haven decided to stay on the island together.

Though some were much more receptive to welcoming Survivors than others.

# GRACE

### SATURDAY, APRIL 22
### 11:10 A.M.

THE FLIGHT TO HAVEN is only thirty-two minutes from take-off to landing.

Captain Gregory Finnegan, the pilot, tells Grace to sit back and relax as he fires up the panel of controls that Grace can see from her seat. Although the plane can hold six passengers, she is the only one on board besides the captain.

Once the plane seems level and cruising, Grace pulls her earbuds out of her pocket, the same pocket as her mask, and plugs them into her ears, then taps her phone screen to life.

"Excuse me, sir...uh...Captain?" Grace doesn't know if she should interrupt him while flying or how loudly she should speak. Usually confident and self-assured, she's frustrated with how awkward she feels.

"You can call me Finn," the captain says, glancing back at Grace just long enough to flash a smile. "Everybody does. But if you're gonna ask about beverage service, I'm afraid my flight attendant is off today."

Grace looks around at the small plane and realizes he's kidding. She smiles and lets out a breath, that she didn't realize she was holding, and relaxes a tiny bit for the first time in what feels like weeks.

"I was just wondering if I could use my phone in airplane mode to watch a video," she says.

"No problem," says Finn, now refocused on their skyward route. "Just hope it's not a movie you want to see the end of, because we'll be there before ya know it."

Finn is a handsome older man; older than Grace anyway. If his salt-and-pepper hair is any indication, he's maybe fifty-something. He looks exactly the part of a small-town pilot in his thick leather jacket and faded jeans, and he smells of soap or shaving cream. His light brown eyes, the color of maple syrup, were kind and calm when he welcomed her on board. As if to say, "Don't worry, you're safe with me."

Grace wonders if everyone on Haven usually has this affable, pleasant vibe. And she feels a pang of guilt again for being the first to invade their space.

On her phone, she presses the arrow that brings a Haven file to life.

She wants to continue watching footage of Mayor Irish and the snippets of their town. She wants to feel comfortable with Ruby, so Ruby's comfortable with her. And then maybe the rest of the Haveners will follow the mayor's lead.

# RUBY AND JACK

As easy as Jack's amazing wife is to love, Ruby Irish can be difficult to live with.

While they have both always been early risers, Jack to catch the morning fish and Ruby to catch the breaking news, Jack was beginning to think his wife wasn't sleeping at all. No matter how early he set his alarm, she was up with her coffee and CNN. And when he went to bed, she was still scouring at her computer.

He had always respected his wife for her dedication to her work, but she was taking it as a personal mission to keep everyone safe and healthy. Of course, that was impossible with the power of this disease.

As much as Jack loved Haven, he worried Ruby's job was taking its toll, and he wished he could just repair things to the way they were before.

IT WAS THE SUMMER OF Ruby's college sophomore year, visiting Haven with her parents, when she met the only son of Frank & Sons Hardware Store.

When Frank Irish opened the business ten years earlier, he and Jack agreed to add multiple "Sons" to the name. Partly to honor the children Frank and Iris had lost, and also to give the store a family-friendly edge on the competition. Although, there was never any competition. And everyone knew there was only Jack.

Jack was always mature for his age with a problem-solving mind. He found out, in therapy, that his increased obsession with fixing things was a response to his shitty home life. Carol, his psychologist, had praised Jack for channeling his energy productively rather than into unhealthy alternatives.

Jack would rather have spent time with friends, but he was scared to bring anyone home when he lived with his dad in Ohio. His childhood had been a bleak, lonely place after he lost his mom, and he missed her with a deep, heavy, constant ache. When his dad suggested they move to Haven, Jack was all for a new beginning.

Life improved immensely for Jack immediately after they arrived. With so few kids in the small island school, the students were always excited to see a new face show up in class.

Still awkward, but showing promise, Jack's dark hair, blue eyes and dimples made him crush-worthy material with the girls. And the boys were impressed by his free-throw.

By the end of the first month, he found the kind of friendships with Carl Carson and Todd Walker that he had always envied back home. And Charlotte Chapman had claimed him as her boyfriend, because they walked together to school.

Jack helped his dad at the store, but his true passion was fishing with friends. He combined the two by becoming adept at repairing boats and learning how to sail. The teak he refinished in the hot summer sun attracted a shit-ton of bee stings, but also some steady business and a decent amount of cash.

And his "office" had an incredible view of teenage girls in bikinis.

Once Jack painstakingly refurbished his dad's Tartan to better-than-new, he started his sailing business and knew he'd found his groove. But the real money was in fishing charters. There was only so much t-shirt shopping and fudge-eating that tourists could do on Main Street. And those who stayed for more than a few days liked the variety of getting off-shore.

After several more years of working and saving, Jack bought his first flybridge boat, a 28-foot Luhrs that was modest, but well-equipped. And he got his name on the tourist map.

THE COLLINS FAMILY was spending a week at a Haven rental in July, like they had done every year for a decade, when Mr. Collins suggested they mix things up with a half-day fishing charter. This didn't appeal to his wife and daughters, except for Ruby, the most outdoorsy of the bunch, who felt bad for her dear old dad.

At twenty, Ruby was old enough to realize Haven-on-the-Lake was not a cheap vacation. Her dad had been footing the bill all these years, without a single request of his own. "If my girls are happy, I'm happy," he would say. But he deserved to be happier.

They only needed a small boat for the two of them, and the name *Irish 4 Fish! Charters* made Ruby laugh. Captain Jack Irish said he could take them out anytime.

While first mate, Todd, helped a bikini-and-cutoffs clad Ruby on board, Jack tried to conduct business as usual. But once the boat was safely out of the marina and he could fire up the throttle, it was hard to stay focused on his job.

With her face tilted up to the sun, and auburn waves rippling in the wind, Jack was mesmerized by Ruby Collins.

Ruby proved to be a natural fisherwoman without a hint of squeamishness. Her casts were strong and smooth, and she quickly lost patience waiting for Jack or Todd to replenish her hook with crickets, grasshoppers, and chunks of raw carp used for bait. She handled the baiting herself and caught even more fish than her dad.

By the end of the day, everyone's skin was pink, the cooler was full, and Ruby was hooked on the sport.

She talked her dad into going out twice more before the end of the week. On the last night, Jack invited her to join a few of his friends at Charlie's Bar, a local favorite. Charlie's was the least charming watering hole at the end of the strip, with its vinyl stools, Formica tables, and a crappy jukebox. But the beers were cheap and the dart games fierce.

Ruby made Jack laugh with her straight-shooting banter and horrible aim, which didn't deter her competitive streak. Much like fishing, she was determined to master darts in record time. By the end of the night, they made a plan to meet back the next summer and resume their competition.

But the next year, Ruby didn't show.

As a journalism major, it was a big deal to land the job of Features Editor for her college paper. Ruby scored the position her junior year. She had also gotten two freelance pieces in a couple of major papers and was eager to see more in print. Her goal was to have her own column someday, and then become a novelist...when she had gathered enough stories to tell.

She told Jack this in her occasional letters. But he wasn't much of a pen pal, responding only with a few short lines on Haven postcards. Ruby stopped writing under the assumption he wasn't interested. And Jack figured he blew it.

The following year, after Ruby graduated from college, she rejoined the family trip before heading off to Philly for an internship that actually paid a few bucks. Not exactly her dream job, but she had a friend on-staff, and he said one of the writers was planning a move to New York.

Ruby went to Charlie's her first night in Haven. The bar was crowded, but not her sisters' style, so they ditched her for The Flying Pig. Ruby waited.

Jack showed up late — windblown, tan, and a few beers in, after a night cruise with friends. He didn't see Ruby at first, so she had the bartender serve him up a glass full of darts "from the fiery redhead at the end of the bar."

"Hey, you're the girl he brought in here last summer," the petite brunette bartender said. She couldn't be much older than Ruby.

"Actually, it was two years ago," Ruby said.

"Oh, okay, yeah, the summers all run together here," said the bartender. "I played darts with you and Jack Irish. Jack was great. You were terrible."

"Well, you never get a second chance to make a first impression," Ruby said, smiling. "Glad mine was stellar."

"Sorry," the bartender said with a laugh. "It's just that Jack always beat everyone at darts and took his champion status seriously. But, you…"

She tilted her head with more recognition and pointed the glass of darts in her hand toward Ruby.

"You made him laugh," she said. "I remember wondering who you were because I could tell he really liked you. I've known Jack since the eighth grade. Even had a crush on him for a while. All the local girls did. But he never looked at any of us the way he looked at you that night."

"I'm Ruby," Ruby said, extending her hand across the bar. "Ruby Collins."

"Charlotte," the girl said, returning Ruby's handshake. "But people call me Charlie."

"Charlie? As in…" Ruby nodded to the glowing sign on the wall behind the bar. "*The* Charlie?"

"Yep," Charlie said. "My dad bought the bar when I was a kid. Our last name is Chapman. Yes, I'm Charlie Chapman. One bad joke away from the silent movie star. My parents thought that was so clever. Anyway, Dad named the bar after me, hoping I'd run it someday. And, well, here I am."

"Well, it's nice to meet you Charlie," Ruby said, then pointed at the dart glass. "Think Jack will remember me?"

"Oh, hell yeah, he'll remember you," Charlie said with a wink and then delivered the goods.

Jack and Ruby were inseparable the rest of the week. Ruby worked as an honorary second mate on the boat. For dinner, they dined with her family at restaurants Jack couldn't afford. Then, they hit the locals' bar circuit of Charlie's, Saxby's Back Room, Spinnaker's Rooftop, The Flying Pig for music…or Rounds, if Dottie was performing.

Ruby loved hearing stories of what it was like to live full-time in the close-knit community of Haven. How they all went full-speed ahead six months a year, working 16-hour days, often at two and three jobs, and barely seeing each other at all. And then, in winter, leaning on each other like family. Balancing lacks and surpluses, finding any excuse to celebrate, and fueling their two-team hockey rivalry with Sunday morning matches. And there was plenty of romance and drama to keep life interesting.

After the third night, Ruby would head back with Jack to his cabin in the woods, where they exercised a fair amount of self-control at first. But...well...they were twenty-somethings in love, after all.

RUBY FOUND OUT SHE was pregnant six weeks after she moved to Philly.

By then, her internship had led to a staff position. And she first chalked up the nausea to stress, long hours, and new foods. But, logically, she knew, even before she took the test.

She had dated guys on-and-off through the years, but nothing serious. She went off the Pill her junior year of college and used other methods when necessary. She and Jack had used condoms. But no stores on the island were open all night. Or in the early morning of her last day in town.

She and Jack had stayed in touch by phone, with hopes for a reunion soon. But Ruby was busy, Jack didn't push, and plans were never confirmed.

She didn't tell Jack about the baby right away. Instead, she gave it another two weeks, weighing all her options and scenarios:

Many babies didn't make it past the first trimester.

Ruby's father had been adopted, and she knew she could make another family very happy.

Ruby was perfectly capable of raising a baby on her own.

OR...

Well, she knew she couldn't handle the other alternative.

But there were two other factors involved that Ruby couldn't ignore. And they were the same reasons why Ruby didn't have boyfriends the last two years in college.

The day she set foot on Jack's boat two years before, she had started to fall in love.

And now, she was also in love with Haven.

When she finally called to tell him the news, Jack had two responses.

"Well, the town could use a decent newspaper."

And, "Marry me."

PAUL JONATHAN IRISH was born seven months later. Followed closely by Georgia, and later, Kade and Declan. All while Ruby was creating The Haven Gazette and penning a series of well-received novels about life in a small island town.

She finally had stories to tell.

Jack's fishing charter business grew over the years. And he staffed three small boats for Havenly Sails Lessons and Leisure. He made a decent living, adored his wife, loved being a dad, and was now close to his own father, who was fifty years sober in February.

Ruby and Jack's whole life was on Haven. Now that their son Declan was home again, everything seemed right with their world. And then the virus hit.

It was Paul who suggested they shut down the airport in November. Although his brothers had teased him about being obsessive and paranoid, Ruby knew how brilliant he was. She also knew he only had Haven's best interests in mind. He was always trying to find ways to increase tourism, improve profits, and keep the town on the map. So when Paul suggested they close the borders, Ruby knew he had done his homework.

OF COURSE, SHE WAS met by resistance from islanders and mainland property owners who had holiday and winter plans. But Ruby held her ground and presented Paul's most grim statistics to ground Haveners in reality. Along with Paul's incredible knowledge, and her own gut instinct that was rarely wrong, she had no doubt quarantining the island was the logical thing to do.

By February, the island's older citizens were saying Ruby had saved their lives. The other residents had come around, too. But Ruby claimed she was only doing what was right to keep their city safe.

And if they were going to thank anyone, it should be her oldest son.

# PAUL

Paul Irish had always been a nerd. And he was perfectly okay with that.

He was a gifted, extraordinary child — and it wasn't just his parents who thought so. He spoke full paragraphs by age two and asked philosophical questions before three. At twenty-nine months, he skeptically inquired: "Who is God's Dad?" And was convinced, when he looked at the stars, that there was "definitely life out there." By four, he could reel off geographical, cosmological, and scientific facts that would make a mint on Jeopardy.

But Paul had a particular affinity for history. Specifically, that of his own town. He took it as a personal challenge to learn everything there ever was to know about Haven-on-the-Lake. Not only from what was written, but also from The Majestic's concierge, Robert Zaggat, who served as the island's official historian.

Paul's first-grade class had gone on a field trip to tour The Majestic, as the island's largest and oldest hotel. It was an imperial, white-columned colossus perched at the highest point on Haven. There were no large hills to speak of, but The Majestic's five-story height gave it the illusion of Atlantis rising up from the sea.

Among the hotel's many notable attributes, it boasted the title of having the second longest porch in the world. Only ten feet shorter than The Grand Hotel of Mackinac Island, Michigan.

For years, it was rumored The Majestic (Paul never shortened it to "Madge") would add the eleven feet to overtake the record. But it was suspected The Grand would add on to theirs...and when would the battle end? Instead, The Majestic added a 201$^{st}$ rocking chair to surpass The Grand's chair total by one. Everyone seemed to be happy with that compromise, but Paul thought they should go for the porch record.

Never mind that nonsense, though, he wasn't there for the chairs. Paul had been counting down the days for the 11 a.m. presentation by the island historian in the hotel orchestra hall. The teacher had promised Mr. Zaggat would give "a detailed and colorful talk on the rich and exciting background of their great and beautiful island."

And Robert Zaggat did not disappoint. Paul was enthralled — then obsessed.

As soon as he was old enough to ride his bike around town unsupervised (which on Haven was age seven or eight), Paul found the secret entrance to the hotel lobby so he could sneak into all of Mr. Zaggat's presentations. Every day at 4 p.m., guests were invited to enjoy a one-hour talk about the history of The Majestic, the island of Haven, and various myths and legends about landmarks, milestones, and people who had come and gone.

Paul was an old soul like his father, with coke-bottle glasses that made his green eyes look buggish, and fair skin that never tanned. Even though their name wasn't truly Irish, Ruby

Collins was, and Paul took his moniker to the extreme with a head full of bright orange waves. He knew he wasn't cute, so he chose to be eccentric.

His idol, Robert Zaggat, wore bow ties every day, which Paul thought to look dignified and smart. So, from the time he was eight years old, Paul requested that "Santa" fill his stocking with a new wardrobe of ties every Christmas. Even in the hottest months, he could be spotted wearing a short-sleeved button-down with a stiff yet jaunty bow at his throat.

After a couple of seasons attending Mr. Zaggat's talks, Paul was disappointed to find that they didn't change much from week to week, or even year to year, because the audience was in constant rotation. Zaggat had the same corny schtick and script for every new incoming group. Sure, he changed it up once in a while, but not enough for Paul's inquiring mind.

Once Paul memorized the standard seven speeches, and a few extras Zaggat threw in for good measure, he was more compelled than ever to investigate facts of his own.

By age twelve, Paul had a head chock-full of historical trivia, and became the youngest ever island tour guide with Haven Carriage Tours. He also volunteered at the Tourism Bureau, the town library, and worked at Haven's only bookstore, Island Reads, on Main. He wrote a column for The Haven Gazette, the newspaper his mother had started, and constantly found "new" material of old island stories to share.

Paul felt forced to go away to school, because that's what his parents expected, but only lasted two years at Gettysburg College before returning to take over Bob Zaggat's presentations when he retired at 75.

For decades, the island's only modes of transportation were horses, carriages, bicycles, and, of course, by foot. Then, in a highly controversial mid-1990s decision, golf carts replaced horses as the island's second most popular ride, next to bikes. Paul was furious about the golf cart transition and refused to demean himself by "orating the fascinating history of our island's noble landmarks from the white vinyl seat of a glorified toy."

But his prevailing mission to educate tourists about his beloved city got the best of him. So Paul created an extensive collection of audio tours that could be played through the stereo system of his family's two private golf carts, and a couple he used on loan until he could afford his own.

Customers renting the vehicles simply pressed PLAY before they left the Main Street lot and were provided with turn-by-turn directions and a detailed tour of their choice: Historical Haven, Haven Hotels, Havenly Homes, A Taste of Haven (the restaurant tour), Haven Highlights, Havenly Views, Haven Hot Spots, and the conciliatory Island Pub Crawl.

The pub crawl was Paul's least favorite tour, but one of his biggest money-makers — despite the dents and accidents those customers usually caused.

By the end of its first season, Haven Hear-n-Steer Self-Driven Tours became one of the most popular tourist attractions on the island and Paul's primary source of income. But he would still tell you he preferred the horses.

Even though Paul's bright hair had deepened to a thick, dark auburn, and his dad's stately features transformed him from nerd to handsome scholar, Paul never showed interest in dating. He knew it was not-so-secretly speculated, over the years, that he was gay. And his mother made a point to defend all sexual preferences, if the topic ever came up. She was an early adopter of the mantra "Love is love."

But the truth was, Paul, with his big, busy, overstuffed brain, preferred to keep the rest of his life as uncomplicated as possible. And when the internet finally came to the island, he became a self-professed computer geek. He had finally found some worthy, intellectual company.

He used the technology to expand his business, along with many others on the island, and was constantly finding ways to give the Tourism Bureau a boost. He most recently created an app called Havenly Headquarters and Help ($H^3$) that was a one-stop source for everything from an interactive island map to same-day grocery delivery. And, of course, there were extensive links to learn about Haven's history and facts.

PAUL'S KNOWLEDGE OF all-things-internet was what led him to the discovery of the mysterious illness that was ransacking Asia and, he believed, would soon transform the world.

He secretly ordered enough masks and gloves to protect local residents from each other. And even a couple hazmat suits, for extreme emergency. (Plus, it was a good excuse to finally own a hazmat suit.) But none of that gear would do squat if Haven opened its docks to the illness.

By mid-November, when Paul had gathered enough information to make him *not* look paranoid or insane (even though his jughead brothers would say otherwise), he presented the facts to his mother and advised her on what to do.

He knew Declan was coming home for Thanksgiving, and Paul texted him to bump up his dates, but of course his carefree brother had more adventures planned. So Paul used the time to scour the news for signs of the disease in the U.S.

He found reports of mysterious respiratory flus popping up all over American towns. No one was putting it together that the virus was already here. But once he found undeniable proof, he convinced his mom to act. He used worst-case scenarios and the bleakest reports to help her scare the Haveners shitless, until they stopped balking and canceled their plans.

When all hell broke loose on the mainland, the islanders hailed Paul a hero, but he knew it would be short-lived. The virus was still coming to Haven and their only hope was to control the speed.

Paul was originally in favor of becoming an Immunity Community. It was the best way to protect Haven, if they had to open their docks. But being the government's first location wasn't Paul's optimal choice.

The tests were still too new, for both the virus and antibodies. Also, more secondary illnesses, particularly those in kids, were popping up every day. He worried about his sister's son, Jax, and his already-compromised lungs. A city without a decent hospital was not where that kid should be. Paul thought, if he was his sister, he would get out of here fast.

But Paul had other demons to fight, and Georgia could take care of herself.

# GEORGIA

Paul was two years old when Georgia came along. And she was everything Paul wasn't. The light, breezy, bouncy balance to Paul's impassive demeanor.

Georgia had inherited the Irish family traits in the most adorable ways. Strawberry blonde ringlets framed her heart-shaped face, and just the right smattering of freckles sprinkled her turned-up nose. She had the same green eyes as Paul, but Georgia didn't need glasses, so they were in perfect proportion to the rest of her face. And, of course, she had the dimples that turned her adorability up to ten.

Without any persuasion from her unpretentious mother, Georgia had a fondness for fashion — with sequins, tutus, and whimsical tights as her go-to style choice. As a little girl, she could be found toddling behind Ruby on Main Street, glittering in cuteness and pushing a tiny stroller of impeccably dressed dolls. She was obsessed with creating elaborate wardrobes for any toy (and some pets) that could wear clothes.

When Georgia was gifted a sewing machine at age ten, she took her fashion designs to a whole new level. She started making clothes for herself out of vintage pieces she found at The Holey Moly, the Catholic church's version of a Goodwill store. And though her early creations could best be described as *interesting*, Georgia definitely had a talent.

While most girls her age impatiently awaited womanly curves to fill out tight jeans and bikinis, Georgia was content with the tall, lanky frame she inherited from her mom. She was her own live mannequin and model, often pestering Paul to take pictures of her edgy new looks. But her brother rarely complied. Georgia may have been the first to master the art of the selfie, with a Canon point-and-shoot camera.

She was stylish, popular, and self-assured, which intimidated the boys her age. So Georgia had an on-again-off-again relationship with Matthew Maxwell (of Maxwell's Fudge) from age fourteen or so. Matt was two years older, in Paul's graduating class, and not completely sold on going into his family's business. But he also volunteered at the fire department after graduation, which was enough to keep him on Haven.

Matt had been a cute, floppy-haired kid, who grew into rugged, chiseled, hot "July" in the annual firefighters' calendar. Together, they were a great looking couple, but the textbook example of opposites attracting. He was the playful, gregarious balance to Georgia's goal-oriented resolve, which was what turned them on and off more times than anyone could count.

Determined to go to a prestigious fashion school (Parsons, Pratt or FIT — all in New York), Georgia held as many jobs as possible from the moment she could work. She was a cashier at her grandpa's hardware store, an assistant in Dottie's gallery, a deckhand for her dad, and a server at several restaurants — including The Majestic's Main Dining Hall, which was usually reserved for college students.

Although she preferred the more laid-back vibe of nearly every other restaurant on Haven, Georgia was enamored by Madge's wealthy, high-fashion clientele. All boys and men were required to wear a jacket and tie for dinner, and dresses or dress slacks were required for women. Georgia, who could spot Prada, Versace, Gucci, and the latest Helmut Lang from across the room (and estimate the price of each ensemble) was inspired by what she saw at work — and filtered it into her own designs. She would often stay up for hours after her shifts concocting new creations.

After graduation, although it would be a financial stretch, Georgia followed her dream to Greenwich Village, and pursued a degree at Parsons School of Design.

Even the busiest day of the busiest season on Haven could not have prepared Georgia for life in New York City. It was buzzing, booming, and overpriced...on steroids. And Georgia loved it all.

The city and the school peeled away layers of her talents that revealed courage and creativity she didn't know she had. The critiques were harsh and the competition ruthless, but that only fueled Georgia more. She was no stranger to working hard on little to no sleep.

It was the people, though, that Georgia had trouble warming up to. Turns out, years of serving Chilean Sea Bass to Gucci-clad middle-aged women at The Majestic could not have prepared Georgia for living with their daughters. Everywhere Georgia looked, vanity was glaring, insecurity ran deep, and sincerity was rare. But then, in her second semester Drawing class, Georgia met Mia Holm.

Mia was tiny, barely 5'2", with porcelain skin, ever-changing hair colors, and the plucky, brave confidence of an artistic genius. Students envied her, instructors favored her, and if someone didn't like her designs, Mia always had, oh, only about ten million more in her sketchbook.

Georgia was the mission-driven yin to Mia's adventurous yang, which made them a fearless pair. They went on horrid double dates, drunken shopping sprees, and put hundreds of miles on Mia's VW Bug to follow their favorite, obscure bands...which landed them on stage more than once.

By Georgia's third year, she had grown into a beautiful young woman with a graceful confidence. She was tall and elegant with long auburn waves that never failed to turn heads. And she had the same bright, clever wit that Jack had loved about Ruby.

Georgia was also a knowledgeable New Yorker, able to fire off landmark directions, restaurant suggestions, and subway routes like a Manhattan native. But she was frustrated with her feelings about living in New York. She loved everything about the city, but wasn't *in love* with it, like she had always imagined. Before she moved there, Georgia had fantasized about adoring NYC with the passion of those born-and-raised. She thought its energy would course through her veins, its cultures would make her worldly, and she would transform into a living mosaic of all its slick and jagged pieces. But Georgia still just felt like...herself, only tired all the time.

Sure, she did look the part. More often than not, her massive waves were piled high on her head in an unruly updo that looked both glamorous and laissez faire. Her trademark accessories were black cat-eye sunglasses, deep burgundy lipstick, and a ridiculously long grey knit scarf that she could wrap around her neck three times. She also had a penchant for old jeans and glamorous coats, which she bought at consignment shops. If forced to describe her style, Georgia would call it grunge-meets-Dior, and she pulled it off beautifully.

When strolling the streets of Haven in the off-season, Georgia certainly stood out among the poufy down jackets, fur-and-flannel trapper hats, and practical Sorrells. But once she stepped on the island, she would feel more at home in a minute than in all her years in Greenwich Village.

Whereas New York was a wild party, Haven was a welcoming hug. And when Georgia let herself admit it, she was homesick for her island town. She just kept hoping it was a feeling she would eventually outgrow.

GEORGIA WAS EXHAUSTED from a particularly grueling semester, and in the homestretch toward finals, when Mia dragged her to Wood's Pub for "just one drink" on a Tuesday night. Mia's cousin, Aleksander, had moved to New York from Denmark, and Mia was dating his roommate, Brad. Georgia had been so busy, she hadn't met the cousin yet. And she had the uncomfortable feeling that Mia was trying to set them up.

Alek, a tall and slender blonde, with sharp cheekbones and a chin dimple, looked equally as disinterested to be shoved toward Georgia as she was to meet him. Mia and Brad flitted off to get the first round (aka: make out at the bar) and left the two strangers alone within sixty seconds of being introduced.

Georgia and Alek exchanged idle chit-chat, but the vibe felt awkward and wrong. Thirty minutes and two drinks later, Georgia decided to pull the rip cord. She blamed her exhaustion for her lack of social skills, apologized to Mia and Aleksander, and announced she was heading out. Alek looked relieved and offered to walk her home, since he was heading in the same direction.

"Well that was a nightmare, aye?" Alek had said, wrapping his brown scarf around his neck in defense of the crisp spring night air. "No offense to you. I mean, you're lovely and all, but we were obviously only invited to add some dignity to…well…what I believe you Americans refer to as a booty call?"

This made Georgia laugh. And relax.

"Yes!" She said, buttoning her coat to the top. In Mia's rush to get to the bar, Georgia had forgotten her favorite scarf. "I cannot tell you how many times Mia has dragged me out for 'just one drink.' At midnight. And then has her tongue down some guy's throat before I get even my coat off. I mean, no offense to Brad. I'm sure he's special. What *they* have is *obviously* a true connection of souls."

Alek's laugh was loud and genuine.

"Ah, yes," he said. "This would explain why Norah Jones has been playing on a continuous loop in our flat as Brad leans his head against our rain-soaked window, counting the seconds until he sees Mia again."

Their banter came fast and easy after that. Alek asking Georgia how she ended up in New York. Georgia learning that Alek had planned to play professional soccer until a knee injury took him out his last year of Gymnasium (Denmark's version of high school).

Alek's family owned a small but popular hometown bakery where he had worked most of his life. Taking over the business was a natural Plan B. A humdrum, lackluster, soul-crushing Plan B. He did like to cook, but he would rather be a chef. Alek used the excuse of wanting to expand the business as his reason to study in New York.

And now, although he didn't necessarily want to plant roots in America, he dreaded more than ever serving life baking bread in Denmark.

Georgia had shared his sentiment about not falling in love with New York in the way she thought she would, but confessed that she felt the opposite about returning home. She was looking forward to going back for the summer.

Georgia tried to describe the easy comfort of her family and friends, the lively adrenaline of tourist season, and the interesting variety of two or three jobs. She told him how much she loved the excitement and buzz of local and temporary worker-bees coming together at the end of each night...slap-happy, horny, and young. And she realized, again, how much she adored her Haven.

Alek said it sounded like the most perfect balance of people and life and love that any city could ever be.

"Coincidentally," he'd said, taking off his scarf and laying it behind Georgia's neck, then crossing and tucking oh-so-carefully to protect her from the cold. "My last name actually means small island."

He said he hoped to see Haven-on-the-Lake someday. And Georgia was surprised at how much she wanted him to.

It wasn't until they bid farewell at the corner of 7th and Greenwich, after chatting until well past two, that Georgia realized her apartment wasn't on Alek's way home at all.

AND NOW...FIFTEEN YEARS, one stone-church wedding, a five-star bistro, a boho boutique, and three toe-headed children later...Georgia and Alek Holm are faced with the decision to stay on Haven or go.

Alek is diabetic, a condition he has managed since childhood. Nine-year-old Jax has asthma. And their daughter, Zoey, is barely one.

Georgia has been glued to the television and internet since her mother broke the news three weeks before, and she can hardly stand to learn another virus-related thing. At the time of the announcement, China was still in full lockdown, Italy was running out of room to store their dead, New York and L.A. hospitals were completely overwhelmed, and they weren't even at the top of the curve.

In the weeks that followed, the world has only gotten worse. Children who had the virus are now sick again several weeks later. People with no pre-existing conditions are dying from the disease. And at a recent Survivors Freedom Alliance protest, one guy shot three people.

Georgia doesn't believe it's possible for a hundred percent of the Survivors coming to Haven to be hundred percent cured. She has read too many stories about tests, mistakes, and fatal relapses. She knows people hide their sickness to work and travel and rebel. She believes it's only a matter of time before some idiotic, dishonest "Survivor" — or two, or three, or ten — will stifle their relapsing symptoms long enough get on the ferry and contaminate the entire island.

But where should her family go? Should they stay home on Haven, a plane ride away from any major hospital? Isolate themselves on the mainland away from family and friends? Or go seek refuge in Denmark, where the virus is minimal for now? They would have no income there, and Alek's parents have passed.

Georgia and Alek have decided to stay on Haven for now. And today, as the first Survivor is on her way to town, Georgia is doubting herself again for the hundredth time this month.

It breaks her heart to feel that she's no longer safe at home.

# GRACE

SATURDAY, APRIL 22
11: 30 A.M.

CAPTAIN FINNEGAN WAS right when he'd said the flight would be over before she knew it. Grace slips her phone in the pocket of her laptop bag, and watches the island come into view.

Even from a distance, she can see The Majestic Hotel commanding the western landscape like a gleaming white palace among the grey-brown trees.

There are plenty of evergreens, too, but the island still seems weeks away from spring, even though calendar declared it over a month ago. Grace imagines that when the last wave of Survivors arrive, Haven-on-the-Lake will be in full bloom. Their first impression will be lovely and flowery and bright. Much more welcoming than the prickly branches greeting her today.

As the plane gets closer, Grace sees the island's storybook appeal and can feel its potential for magic. She imagines the romances, weddings, and magnificent events that had taken place there over the last hundred years.

A church stands alone, not far from The Majestic, its pointed steeple reaching high for the sky. To its east, and along the whole southern coast, two strips of buildings line a grey, paved road. Main Street. Grace recognizes it from the map she pulled up online in her motel room the night before.

As the landing gear rumbles beneath her feet, Grace tightens her seat belt and takes a deep breath. Letting it out slowly, she counts to five, to let her anxiety go. The panic attacks that came with her diagnosis are fewer and farther between, but still erupt at inopportune times. And she doesn't need one today.

She reaches in her pocket for her mask, inclined to put it on, as is a habit now whenever she connects with people. But she's not required to wear it anymore, because Haveners never have.

How bizarre, Grace thinks, that *they're* the oddities now — people unguardedly breathing the same air, sharing their personal space, coming and going as they please. While the rest of the world is standing six feet apart, they're facing this side by side.

She wonders if that will make it easier or harder to come in contact with people like her. And, for the first time since she got the assignment, Grace wishes she wasn't alone. She will be the only Survivor on Haven this week…and she's starting to feel like a freak.

*Poised, professional, prepared*, she repeats to herself again and again, trying to feel older and wiser than her twenty-eight roller coaster years.

But as the captain announces that they're about to land, she reaches for her mask one last time. Rubbing it like a good luck charm, she hopes she'll make at least one friend among the Haveners. Or else it will be a very lonely two months.

# KARA

### SATURDAY, APRIL 22

THE PARTY LAST NIGHT was perfect. Well, perfect-ish. A much-needed reprieve from the horrible stuff going on all over the world….and now all the stress on Haven.

Kade and Macy, Kara's best friend since high school, had done a beautiful job decorating the bar for her birthday. She knew they put even more effort than usual into it because it was the last big blast before the Survivors arrive. But Kara was okay with pretending all the fuss was for her.

After one too many margaritas on an empty stomach, Macy confessed that she and Kade had gone on a covert mission the night before to commandeer the town's Christmas lights from the basement of the Island Pointe Hotel.

"Wait, so maybe they're The Pointe's Christmas lights then?" Macy had said, obviously giving more thought to the details after-the-fact than when the heist was taking place.

"The Pointe isn't open in the winter," Kara reminded her. "Anyway, how'd you get in? CJ?"

Carl Carson, Jr. is one of Haven's only two winter police officers, and also serves as the night watchman for, well, pretty much the whole town. There's not much to watch this time of year. Unless you count CJ's hopelessly devoted gazes at Macy. He has had a crush on her since she moved to Haven in sixth grade, when her mom and dad joined the family business, Maxwell's Fudge. Macy comes from fudge money.

"No! We broke in!" Macy said, eyes dancing at the excitement of it all. "Kade jiggered open a basement window. Then he slid in and helped me down. You would not believe what they had down there! I'm pretty sure they've kept *everything ever* since the hotel opened. Furniture, bikes, appliances. Golf carts! From, like, the very first year they were invented. And they still had their whole 4th of July float down there! Hulk's head scared the crap out of me."

The parade theme had been superheroes last year.

Kara wondered if Haven would have a parade this summer now that everything would be different, and all the regulars would be replaced by strangers. But she batted the thought from her mind, scolding herself for breaking her own rule. She had told everyone that her only birthday wish was *not* to discuss the virus for the night.

As Macy flitted on about Operation Decoration, Kade's band was setting up on the center stage.

Kara had always thought the whole bar was a clever, cozy design. Everything about it was round; there wasn't a sharp corner in the place. The front windows looked like giant portholes on a ship. The hi-top tables were round. The stage was round. And she especially loved the giant round bar.

Chunky, wooden bar stools allowed about forty patrons to belly up to the weathered counter to watch the pretty bartenders sling drinks and shamelessly flirt. In the high season, Rounds always had the hottest staff on the island, and there was no shortage of exhibitionism — everyone trying to top each other with mixing and pouring tricks. Even when there was no musical entertainment, Rounds was always packed to watch the servers' show.

And, occasionally, customers were treated to a rare performance by Kade's band, which rarely played anymore since he bought the bar.

The band consisted of three members: Kade, Declan, and their buddy, Ryan Oakley, on drums or keyboards, whichever he was in the mood to play. But never both, since the stage was so small.

They called themselves The Oakleys.

The stage was barely big enough for Kade and Deck to walk around Ryan in the center. But after nearly a decade of performances as a trio, the choreography was seamless. Everyone in the audience could get an eyeful of the handsome Irish boys. Neither of whom were either fair or ginger, despite the name. And each their own flavor of eye candy.

Kara had always preferred Kade's dark hair and clean-cut style over Declan's grungy lifeguard look. But they both have the same tropical blue eyes, which can either look like a sea or a storm, depending on the mood. Nobody knows where they got their musicality from, but both can carry a tune. And Kade can shred the guitar.

Even though Deck was in her graduating class, Kara had a crush on Kade since...forever. It was Macy who liked Declan. But Declan dated half the girls on the island, including tourists much older than him. There were never any shortage of scandals at Haven-on-the-Lake.

Kade was three years older than Kara, all natural charm and easy confidence, while Kara was a bespectacled math-trovert. She tutored Declan on everything from fractions to vectors at the Irish family kitchen table for years, in pathetic effort to get a glimpse of Kade — who would simply breeze through with a smile and a "Hey" — at most. And those trademark Irishmen dimples.

But then, there was Isabella. Always Isabella. Paired with Kade like a celebrity duo since the seventh grade. Kade-n-Izzy. Izzy-n-Kade. Bellakade. Kadabella. Haven royalty.

Isabella Flores was one of seven stunning Flores kids whose family owned Cabanas on the north side of town. The tacos were amazing and chorizo burritos to-die-for. When Cabanas got their liquor license, their rating rose to five stars on TripAdvisor and business skyrocketed.

Cabanas expanded from a walk-up taco stand to an indoor-outdoor restaurant. Then, Isabella's two older brothers opened Havenas Salsa Bar on the island's east side. Too secluded for restaurants and too rocky for waterfront homes, the east side of Haven was ideal for blaring music.

As the only dance club in town — which wasn't much more than a covered patio strung with lights and blasting salsa — Havenas was a popular spot in the summer for big-city tourists, middle-aged singletons, and Europeans. Most others preferred the restaurants on Main Street which usually offered live music in the form of guitarists and duos. Or lively bars like Rounds, The Flying Pig, and Spinnaker's, which had great cover bands. Saxby's was known for its jazz.

At Havenas, though, there was Isabella. Graceful, exotic, alluring Isabella. She was an incredible dancer with a genuine smile that made her both sexy and loveable. Women wanted to look like her, men wanted to dance with her.

She would often kick off the night with free lessons, then allow a few sweaty men to hold her tiny, wiggling hips until she slid them into rhythm with a stranger. Once the dancefloor was packed, Isabella would transform into life-of-the-party mode, enticing parched patrons with buckets of cold Coronas, trays of tequila shots, and pitchers of jalapeno-cilantro margaritas — or whatever her bartender brothers would concoct as the special of the day.

Isabella continued to help with the family businesses for a couple of years after Kade left for college, but he came back every holiday and summer to continue their sizzling affair. Finally, Isabella had socked away enough money to join him in New York the fall of his junior year, with hopes to realize her dream of becoming a professional dancer.

She got a couple small jobs in off-off-broadway productions. And then her big break came when she was hired as a back-up dancer for a six-episode variety show to air in the summer. But that didn't last long.

Rumor had it that she hooked up with the married director, ruined her relationship with Kade, and only lasted three episodes.

Isabella was five months pregnant and living back in Haven when the show premiered in July. And all of her scenes had been cut. She never did reveal who the baby daddy was; and quietly resumed employment in the family business, serving tacos at Cabanas.

This all happened the summer before Kara was to leave for college, and she had been counting on seeing Kade again. No longer the gangly brainiac that gawked at him from his kitchen table, Kara was now a blonde-haired, hazel-eyed beauty, with her father's full lips and her mother's full chest that filled out her senior year.

Kara had dated the few cute guys her age on Haven and had some flings with Fudgies (Haven's summer tourists), but her heart always belonged to Kade.

Oh, she was fully aware of how stupid that was. And she felt like an idiot holding out hope for her childhood crush. But maybe, just maybe, he would finally see her as more than her little brother's tutor.

When Kade didn't come home that summer, Kara blamed Isabella.

If she hadn't gotten knocked up and broke Kade's heart, then he would have...he would have what?

He would have still been with Isabella.

Kara wouldn't have him either way. Damn Isabella.

Kara decided it was time to stop being a ridiculous small-town lovesick dreamer and get on with her life. As much as she had always loved Haven — her home since the age of six when her dad took the pilot job — Kara couldn't wait to leave.

And when Kara left, she left. Didn't come back for the summers, like most of her local friends. Instead, she used the excuse that she wanted to pursue two degrees. One in Elementary Education, and one in Graphic Design. Kara had always wanted to teach, but hoped to travel too, and she thought adding a second skill would bring in some extra cash.

Kara spent one summer studying at Oxford in England. And then returned to the U.K. the following year on a work-exchange program. She, her boyfriend, Sam, and four other college friends, shared a two-bedroom apartment near England's Hampstead Heath. Kara and Sam lucked out by getting jobs at the same downtown London pub called The Crispin. Because the bar was in the business district, they had weekends off.

This gave Kara her chance to see more of the world. Or at least where her Eurail pass could take her from Friday to Sunday. Her grand finale of the summer was a "Taste of Europe Tour" when she and Sam ate and drank their way from Amsterdam to Milan.

Kara spent all her earnings, racked up her first credit card debt, and packed on fifteen pounds. Even though she and Sam didn't last past September, it was the best summer of her life.

When she returned to her final year of school, Kara added yoga and running to her growing list of passions.

By the time she graduated, at twenty-three, with two degrees and a yoga instructor certification, Kara felt like the world was full of possibilities. Her immediate plan was to pop back to Haven for the summer and regroup, then decide which dream to follow.

She didn't expect the two bombs that were dropped upon her arrival.

One: Kara's mother had been having a three-year affair with the manager of Spinnaker's North, a man ten years her junior. She was leaving Kara's dad to move to Key West and help him run Spinnaker's South.

Two: Kade Irish had bought Rounds Bar and was moving back to Haven.

Macy Maxwell was already teaching at Haven Elementary and working part-time at her parents' fudge shop when Kara returned to the island. Macy let Kara move into the spare room of her Centerhaven ranch, which she shared with her sister, Marley. (Yes, the Maxwells were one of *those* families. Everyone was an M.) That's where Kara stayed until her mom moved away, late June.

Kara, of course, felt terrible for her dad — a kind, gentle, friendly guy who had been Haven's pilot for seventeen years. Her mother had always been a bit of an introvert, and never seemed to embrace Haven like Kara or her dad did. Or so people thought. Kara now knew that couldn't be further from the truth. Apparently, her mother had been *embracing* some parts of Haven even more.

Kara was still deciding what to do with her life when Rounds held its grand re-opening in July. Kade had been in town for a month at that point, but Kara hadn't been much for socializing. She'd spent most of her days at the Island Pointe pool, where she took a job as a lifeguard. It was easier to save the lives of tourists than survive the pitiful looks of the locals.

But everyone was going to Rounds for what would literally be Haven's party of the century, to date. So, of course, Kara had to attend. She was already more than tipsy when she finally talked to Kade.

At her blondest and tannest ever, Kara didn't have a problem catching his eye when she squeezed her way up to the bar for a drink. Kara simply leaned across the counter in a way that made her cleavage ooze up and out of her deep-cut halter, knowing this could beckon a bartender faster than a hundred-dollar bill.

After being called a beanpole, "Twiggy," and a tomboy most of her life, it had taken Kara a while to navigate the power of her curves. In college, she was alternately shocked and irritated at the silly, stupid reactions to a particularly revealing outfit. But her strong-willed, feminist side wasn't about to let society dictate her wardrobe. There was a fine line between body confident and dick tease, but Kara couldn't care less about who thought of her as the latter. She knew the truth.

Although, on this particular occasion, Kara relished Kade's stare, shock...and embarrassed blush once he realized who she was. As if he'd unknowingly checked out his own sister from behind. But she used this short window of attention to her advantage to congratulate him on taking over Rounds and ask if he could use an extra hand, joking that she was now an international expert at the art of tending bar. He hired her immediately and let her start that night.

Kade and Kara were dating by the end of the week.

In September, Kara took a full-time job teaching at Haven Elementary. It helped that Macy's brother-in-law, Scott, was the principal...and staff turnover was notoriously high since the school and town were so small. If you hadn't grown up on Haven, it could be hard to get used to. If you had, it could be hard to leave.

Kara's dad was thrilled that she decided to stay.

ONE OF THE FIRST STUDENTS Kara ever instructed was Isabella's little boy, Ben. Isabella turned out to be a lovely, helpful parent, though reserved and very private. Kara often wondered if there was more to that story of hers. And Ben never mentioned his dad.

Isabella never posed a threat to Kade and Kara at all. She kept to herself on the north side of the island, working at Cabanas and taking care of her son.

Once Kara and Kade were together, she fell more in love with Kade than she ever imagined possible. She believed their fated story was one that movies were made of. It was only a matter of time before they would get married and have kids of their own.

But as the years went by, Kade seemed content to simply *date*.

Although she stayed at his cabin in the woods more often than her dad's spacious home by the water, Kade never even hinted at them moving in together. Kara was the one who announced, exasperated by living out of a backpack, that she was claiming a dresser drawer.

Kade just shrugged and smiled.

"Mi sock drawer es tu sock drawer," he said, clearing out his belongings in one swift swoop and waving toward the open drawer like a gentleman holding the door. Kara couldn't tell if he was being sweet or patronizing, which was often the case with the Irish family. Sarcasm was their second language, lobbing jokes and jabs around the dinner table like a verbal volleyball game.

Kara took the sock drawer win. And half the medicine cabinet, too. But the exchange had left her unsettled. Was this all she was ever going to get?

Kade's long hours at the bar left Kara with *a lot* of extra time on her hands, so she put her graphic design degree to work. She helped Kade's brother, Paul, with the Tourism Bureau's website and aided many of Haven's businesses with their online presence as well. She also designed t-shirts, which Macy's parents sold exclusively at their fudge shops.

Kara's corny-clever slogans were surprisingly popular with tourists:

> *For Haven's sake...Relax.*
> *Haven a great time on the lake!*
> *A little bit o' Haven is a hell of a lot o' fun!*
> *Everybody wants to go to Haven. And nobody wants to go home.*

It helped that Kade, with his solid, strong, football player physique (if Haven had a team) modeled her creations at the bar.

KADE HAD BEEN WEARING Rounds' custom design — *Cheap Rounds. Great Sounds. A match made in Haven.* — when he and Macy took the stage to sing "Happy Birthday" at Kara's party last night. Macy had an amazing voice, but it took her a few drinks to perform.

The rest of the guests joined the serenade and the party took off from there. Eighty-four people had come, nearly half the town. How many people could say that, no matter where they lived? As much as Kara still loved to travel — and she did in the summertime — she knew there was no place like Haven.

The Oakleys played late into the cold April night and most people stayed until the end.

Even Dottie Kessner made a rare musical appearance with a three-song country set: Patsy Cline's *I Fall to Pieces*, Kenny

Roger's *Ruby Don't take Your Love to Town* (a favorite shout-out to the mayor) and *I Will Always Love You* by Dolly Parton, Dottie's personal idol and ageless doppelganger. Dottie, a living legend of Haven, was still a looker at nearly eighty.

The music was lively. The drinks were flowing. And the night was a dream-come-true.

The only thing that would have made it better was if Kade Irish had proposed.

When he didn't pop the question over the holidays, Kara had thought maybe it would be on her birthday. But then the world changed. Her party was her last smidge of hope.

NOW, SHE WAS WAKING up on the first day of her 28th year to attend Mayor Irish's official announcement that Haven would be opening their docks for this ridiculous Immunity Community. Kara's dad was on his way to the island with the first virus Survivor. And Kara was still not engaged.

Worst. Birthday. Ever.

# GRACE

SATURDAY, APRIL 22
11:40 A.M.

THE RUNWAY LANDING is even and smooth as the wheels touch the ground, and then roll, not far, to a stop. With no jetway extending to the outside of the plane, Grace doesn't know if she should unbuckle, so she waits to be told what to do.

The building she sees out the window is a large, grey metal garage — or a very small airplane hangar. Beyond that is a modest control tower, sprouting from a squat white building with a row of yellow golf carts parked neatly in front of its door. *That's right! There are no cars!*

A guy about her age, thirty or so, wearing a faded red ball cap, slides open the large door of the hangar, and pushes a staircase toward the plane.

"Welcome to Haven," Captain Finnegan announces as he ducks from the cockpit into the cabin. He nods to her lap while snapping on a pair of rubber gloves. "You can unbuckle now. I'll grab your things and then deplane to leave you alone to change."

He opens a small closet door behind the cockpit and pulls out a bright yellow drawstring bag.

"Sorry you have to change clothes in here, but them's the rules!" He shrugs and smiles. "The rest of the folks will be arriving by ferry and there will be larger facilities for them. There's a sink in the back for you to wash your hands."

Even though the Survivors are *supposedly* not contagious (Grace knows Mayor Irish is still skeptical), it's still not completely clear how long the virus can live on surfaces, material, or unwashed skin.

Per the mayor's orders: All Survivors will wash all exposed skin upon arrival and change into clothing provided until their own belongings are washed or cleaned. Nothing from the mainland is to come in contact with Haveners until it is fully sterilized. And this includes human beings.

Survivors are allowed to bring one disposable bag of clothes and a few essential items, which can all be washed or wiped down with a disinfectant cloth. This is all part of the many safety rules that Mayor Irish has now famously demanded.

Grace assumes Captain Finnegan will have to go through the decontamination process as well, since he greeted her in Ohio. Their new normal is only just beginning, and she feels sorry for the Haveners all over again.

"There's a plastic bag in there for the clothes you're wearing." Finn says, nodding to the bag now in Grace's hands. "And I apologize in advance for the t-shirt. Declan Irish, the mayor's son, came up with it. My daughter, Kara, did the artwork. Hope you all have a sense of humor."

He opens the door and steps out, offering a few last directives.

"Just give this lever here a yank to open when you're done; I won't lock it. Ryan will show you where to go next. And then Ruby and Jack Irish will pick you up to take you into town. See you there!"

And then he's gone, shutting the door behind him.

Grace had been asked to supply her clothing sizes on the extensive online forms she filled out the day before, which also informed her of the entry process. Inside the bag is a light blue t-shirt, grey hoodie, black joggers, and black rubber Nike slides.

When she unfolds the shirt, she can't help but laugh:

**I survived the virus
and all I got was this lousy t-shirt...**

And on the back:

**...and a trip to the middle of nowhere.**

Below that is the Haven logo: HAVEN-ON-THE-LAKE in black lettering that forms an island silhouette backed by a gradient sun of pink, orange, and yellow. Pretty.

GRACE CHANGES INTO her Havenwear, noting that the hoodie sports the logo, too. She feels silly and tacky, but physically comfortable, which is probably what the Haveners are going for. It's their island and they want to set the tone.

The young man at the bottom of the steps smiles broadly at Grace as she exits the plane. She wonders if he's being friendly or just laughing at her clothes. He introduces himself as Ryan Oakley and reaches out to shake her hand.

Grace instinctively jolts back and stares at this gesture like he just reached for her boob.

*That's right*, she thinks, *this is normal for them. They've been doing it all along.*

She awkwardly extends her arm...as if it belongs to someone else...and shakes hands for the first time in months.

There are so many new habits she'll now have to break, a whole mindset she'll have to retrain. Like a prisoner emerging from captivity, she'll have to get used to full freedom again. And she's not quite sure how it feels, as her eyes surprise her with tears.

"Grace," she chokes out, willing herself not to cry. "Grace Dawson. It's very nice to meet you, Mr. Oakley. Thank you for having me here."

She has no idea what to say. It's like her social skills have lay dormant, too.

"Oak," he says, with a chuckle and a gap-toothed smile that suits his boyish face well. "Everyone calls me Oak. Here, I'll show you where the Irishes are coming to pick you up."

Grace follows behind him toward the small white building and row of golf cart taxis, which she now sees are artfully painted in various shapes and shades of yellow, with black and white grids here and there — a modern shout-out to classic cabs. She had seen similar taxis in Italy, during her short-lived travel blogger phase. And she realizes that's how she's feeling right now, like a foreigner in a strange, new land.

But she also feels a sense of calm as she breathes in the crisp, cool air that smells of fresh rain and damp cement...with a waft of spearmint, too. Ryan Oakley has slowed his stride, closing the gap of space and scent, and she realizes she is close enough to smell a stranger's gum.

Until then, Grace had been distancing herself from him, at least six feet behind.

*I had no idea how much I missed this*, she thinks, now shoulder-to-shoulder with a man she just met. *Life. People. Connection. How it all was before. And how it's so NOT like this at home.*

Grace has only been on Haven for minutes and already she doesn't want to leave.

# DECLAN

Even though Declan Irish was twelve years younger than his brother, Paul, and delivered by emergency C-section at thirty-four weeks...he was always told he was planned and prayed for. And that was the absolute truth.

It was his older brother, Kade, who had been the big surprise.

RUBY IRISH WAS A YOUNG and energetic mother when she had Paul at twenty-three. Her life had taken an extreme and unexpected detour from the future she thought she charted. But she had fallen in love with Jack, and the captivating magic of Haven, and she was still determined to make her mark on the world. Just now from a different location.

The island's original newspaper, The Haven Herald, wasn't much more than a two-page flyer from June until September. And the editor, Marty Simon, was happy to hand it over.

Marty was the high school English teacher. Gym teacher sometimes, too. And also the owner and handyman of several rental homes. When the houses were full, he was busy with questions. When they were empty, they needed repairs. And from September until early June, he always had papers to grade.

Ruby decided the newspaper needed a complete renovation itself and named her new publication The Haven Gazette. It was still the early eighties, and personal computers weren't commonplace. So Ruby wrote on a typewriter, crafted the layouts by hand, and printed the twelve-page publication on the "new" rubber roller press acquired in the 70s.

She talked Marty into adding journalism projects to his weekly curriculum, and asked the art teacher, Barbara Peters, to incorporate photography into her lesson plans. This gave Ruby a freelance staff that she didn't have to pay.

As Ruby expanded The Gazette, she expanded her family, too. Georgia Charlotte Irish was born when Paul was two, and Ruby was twenty-five. Two kids and a growing newspaper, along with Ruby's passion for writing fiction, kept her life busy and full. Plus, she and Jack still tried to squeeze in date nights or afternoon fishing jaunts whenever the two could slip away. They were content as a family of four, until life had other plans.

PAUL WAS NINE AND GEORGIA was seven, The Gazette had an actual staff, and Ruby's first book had just been published when she was hit with a bout of seasickness on an early October cruise.

Ruby had always been proud of her sea legs and iron, unrockable gut, but the water was choppy that day. She and Jack probably shouldn't have gone out. But the boat provided a spectacular view of Haven's changing leaves. The island looked like a floating fall bouquet just before the long winter greyness set in.

Ruby wanted to get pictures for the paper's next edition, but instead she vomited most of the time. And Jack only got a few blurry shots.

When the nausea repeated itself the next morning, and the next morning after that, it wasn't hard to figure out that rocky waters weren't the cause.

Kade Collins Irish was born the following spring.

The seven years between him and Georgia made Kade her living doll at first. Then, he started to walk and lumber through his Terrible Twos. Georgia announced, through tears more than once, that he wasn't so cute anymore.

Ruby and Jack decided they should probably give Kade a friend.

Ruby never had trouble conceiving before. Paul and Kade had been surprises, and Georgia was the answer to "Think we should try for another?"

But Ruby's thirty-something ovaries weren't as easily controlled. She suffered two miscarriages the first year they tried. And Declan started out as a twin. Two babies at the first ultrasound made Ruby and Jack both gasp in shock, then laugh through happy tears. But an emergency trip to the mainland, after Ruby had spotted and cramped, showed one of the twins had aborted. Ruby was high-risk after that.

Winter on Haven, which was six months long, was a good time to hole up anyway, so the Irish family did.

Paul was self-sufficient by then, usually with a book in his hand. And Georgia was a good little helper, when not screaming at Kade to let go of her dolls.

Jack usually helped his dad in the off-season, with the many building repairs. The boats were shrink-wrapped for the winter and the phone was quiet for early reservations. So he simply rebalanced his time to cook, clean, and take care of the kids.

The Gazette was thin in the winter, but Jack still ensured distribution. With social media still years away, the residents craved connection as they shuttered themselves in from the cold. Recaps of summer highlights, business plans for the following year, and holiday, church, and school events usually filled the off-season issues. Plus, historical stories of the island (which Paul had begun to contribute), family news of births, deaths, and weddings, and the standard classified ads were enough to pad the pages.

Although there was a medical center on the island and several trained EMTs, Ruby couldn't shake the nagging feeling that she should be on the mainland by May $12^{\text{th}}$, two weeks before the baby was due. She made a mental note to call some friends and secure a place to stay.

The second week of April, Ruby woke in the middle of the night to what she thought were more Braxton Hicks contractions. She had been having them since the second trimester, which was early but no cause for alarm. Yet, these were more severe and timing at eight minutes apart.

Ruby had given birth to three babies and knew labor when she felt it. A house call from Dr. Curt Hanson, the island's only MD, validated Ruby's concerns and she went to the clinic for an ultrasound. Results showed the baby to be breech, she was dilated to two, and the baby's inconsistent heart rate was the doctor's biggest concern.

Pilot Brian Ramsay was already on standby at the Haven Airport when Ruby, Jack, and Doc Hanson arrived. Brian was the second call Jack had made. Then one to Dottie and Buck to come and get the kids.

He wasn't sure what was going to happen and didn't want them in the house. "Aunt Dottie" had been their childcare help when Ruby and Jack were busy with work, and it was comforting to know they would be no worse for the wear, no matter how long Ruby and Jack were gone.

Doc Hanson accompanied Ruby and Jack on the thirty minute flight to Rochester, New York, and St. Joe's Hospital was awaiting their arrival. By then, Ruby's contractions were three minutes apart, and she was dilated to five. But this was likely as far as she'd go considering the breech position.

By the time Ruby was transferred to an ambulance on the runway of the Rochester Airport, the baby was in fetal distress with variable decelerations (abrupt decreases in the heart rate) and Ruby was starting to bleed. This meant possible placental abruption, which would threaten the baby's oxygen level. Things needed to happen fast.

Ruby was whisked from the ambulance and into surgery, leaving Jack at the entrance in shock.

"She's in good care" was all Doc could say because "It'll be okay" would sound doubtful and hollow.

As night crept into morning, all Jack could do was pace the sterile halls, which smelled of antiseptic and scrambled eggs, and pray for the lives of his beautiful wife and youngest baby boy. A call to Dottie to check on the kids assured Jack he was not alone. Dottie had activated Haven's emergency phone tree and prayers were being said all over town.

It seemed like hours before the doctor came out, still in scrubs from head to toe, and announced to Jack and Doc that both mom and baby were healthy and doing fine.

To this day, Jack will still say that was the best sentence he has ever heard.

Declan Hanson Irish was born the morning of April 14$^{th}$, weighing 4 pounds 14-ounces, with slick black hair and a bellowing wail that was music to his exhausted mother's ears. Ruby had once read that St. Declan's Stone was the site of many miracles. And a name couldn't be more fitting.

Within weeks, Declan was right on schedule in height, weight, and milestones. His silky dark baby 'do gave way to curls of honey blonde. He was a hybrid of the Irish family trademarks and a few stand-out characteristics of his own. Declan was an early walker, an agile climber, and a fearless daredevil by two. And the kid never knew a stranger; he would go to anyone.

Declan seemed to master any sport he tried as long as it meant he could be outside and on the move. By preschool, the training wheels were off his bike...and it wasn't long before wheelies, then makeshift BMX courses. Ice skating and roller blading were easily mastered, which meant hockey — both ice and street. His free-throw was solid, soccer kick strong, and he broke records with his high jump and sprints.

But Declan was most proud of his skateboarding prowess because that involved the biggest risks. Even though the sport was fading in popularity, Declan found his natural, happy place on that very first skateboard deck (which conveniently became his nickname).

From the minute he received it on his eleventh birthday from Grandpa Frank, Deck was off and rolling. And falling. And flipping. And falling. And kicking and ticking and tacking. And falling and scraping and breaking. The locals used to joke that a cast on Declan's wrist was Haven's official sign of spring. Skateboard season had begun.

Deck, his friends, and his Grandpa Frank would spend hours building ramps and courses on an undeveloped lot in the center of the island. And Deck would get more daring with his stunts each year. By thirteen, he was selling tickets to neighbors for his performances. And the following year, he marketed his ramps to tourists. Teens at the summer rentals could only spend so much time with their folks before they asked to wander off on their own. And that's when Deck would wheel by with flyers to check out *Sk8ter Haven*.

Deck was a talented artist, with a graffiti edge to his work. He not only decorated his ramps, but he refinished old skateboards, too. That was one request to people who visited the Irishes: If you have an old skateboard you were going to toss, please bring it and donate to Deck.

He would then rent the spare boards to tourists in the summer for a dollar per half an hour. And he and his new skater buddies would show off for the teenage girls. Since he used his grandpa's hardware scraps for the ramp construction, everything was a profit. And an entrepreneur was born.

When Declan lost interest in skateboarding, he found more niche businesses to make a buck.

On an island that's less than four square miles, the lack of cars rarely garnered complaints. Most hotels offered a luggage service that transported bags from the ferry so guests wouldn't have to maneuver their Samsonites along the cobblestone walks. When passengers bought their ferry tickets on the mainland, their bag was tagged and delivered to their hotel room within a few hours.

It was Declan who came up with Cartz, the island taxi and luggage service, for those who forgot to check their bags...or simply didn't want to part with their Louis Vuittons.

Since Paul owned a golf cart tourist business and the renters were tough on the vehicles, Declan would revamp the carts Paul couldn't fix. Deck used his creative talents to make each cart a colorful masterpiece. Cartz was not only practical but added an artistic splash to the streets.

And when the ferries were done for the day, Cartz was popular with barhoppers at night. Or simply weary tourists who wanted a stylish taxi ride.

Some of his wealthy passengers asked if the carts were for sale. They would "love to have one for the Florida house" or it would be a hit on their club's private course. Declan was careful to do the math on diminishing his fleet. But if the buyer was willing to wait until fall, it was usually worth the sale. And Deck always had a golf cart stash he could makeover during the winter.

Deck started Cartz at age sixteen, with two carts and a couple of friends. Within a few years it was a thriving business, and he was able to hire a manager to free up his time. As much as he loved cruising tourists around, there was more he wanted to do.

Deck made it clear early on that he had no plans to go to college. He was plenty smart and got decent grades, but he always had one eye on the clock, waiting for the bell to ring.

"Why sit in class for four more years," he said to his folks, more than once. "To work all my life to save money and retire...so I can go to an island and fish? I already do that now. I have already arrived!"

His father could hardly argue. Jack didn't go to college himself. And it would be nice to have someone take over the business, if that's what Deck wanted to do. But he had learned from his own dad not to push, and let Deck make his own decisions.

It wasn't as if Declan lacked motivation to pay his own way in the world. Besides Cartz, he helped on the charter and with the sailing school. He also played in the band with his brother and Ryan. They didn't play often in the summer, but when they did, they packed the house. And Deck was the go-to singer for other venues if their talent didn't show.

He was the friendly, fun, great looking guy that everyone in Haven knew...and the mainlanders came back to see.

With his sun-bleached hair, ever-present tan, and those piercing Irish eyes, Declan never had a problem finding a new girl's heart to break. He made his way through enough of the locals to give him a playboy status. But he maintained friendships with most of his exes, because not only was Deck the life of the party, but he'd give anyone the shirt off his back. (Revealing a pretty damn hot set of abs.)

Besides standard trips to the mainland, Declan showed no signs of leaving Haven until he was twenty-three. Kade had come back to take over Rounds. And even though Deck understood it, he was jealous that his brother got the job.

Kade and the previous owner, Buck, had a special bond. Kade's life had always been like that, falling into things easily.

He was popular, smart, responsible and dated the prettiest girl in Haven. That whole Isabella scandal, when she came back with some other guy's kid, was the only speed bump on Kade's otherwise easy ride. But then he ended up with Kara, who had always said no to Deck.

Declan was aware he was considered the Irish's wild child. Even though he'd been working since he was twelve, he would never command the respect that Kade would have as the owner of the biggest bar in town. Unless he did something bigger.

Most of Deck's other friends had left town for college, and then for jobs. And, though some came back in the summers, Deck was struggling to find his place on Haven. He announced to his family in August that he was heading to Europe for a year.

To leave in the middle of high-season was unheard of for Haveners. But Cartz was being managed by a Maxwell kid, the most wholesome family on the planet. The boats were fully staffed. And even Grandpa Frank had college help.

Declan's plan was to backpack through Amsterdam, Germany, Austria, and Switzerland while the weather was still mild and warm. Then, he'd hit Paris in the fall. After that, his path was open to "whatever appeared under his feet."

His parents supported his choice, but he could see in his mother's eyes that she was worried for her youngest son. And on the night before he left, she told Declan as much.

"You know I've always been proud of you, right?" She said after the rest went to bed and they were sitting alone at the bonfire in the backyard of the family home. "And my biggest hope for you is to be genuinely happy right down to your soul."

"I know, Mom," Deck said. "You don't have to worry about me."

"But...?" Ruby asked.

"But, what?" Deck said.

"There was a 'but' at the end of that sentence, you just didn't say it out loud."

Ruby always had a special connection with her lively, sensitive son. She knew that restless spirit well and the way it sought out new challenges to conquer. She could relate to the struggle of "settling" in a small town, wondering if there was more in the world that you should see and try and do. It was the *shoulds* that kept you up at night when you were a wayward soul.

She also saw how much Deck loved Haven, and she could relate to that, too. They both had true appreciation for this pure and sparkling gem that seemed untouched by the world. She saw how Deck was with the tourists, so proud to show them around. And how loyal he was to the locals, giving jobs to his buddies, pitching in around town, and being the center of connection for his friends whenever they came and went.

But she had seen the envy in her youngest son's eyes when Kade was applauded at the re-opening. And even though that wasn't Deck's dream, he looked lost and out of place. For good reason.

Kade hadn't lived in Haven full-time for eight years. Deck was used to being the star of the show. And now, the spotlight was on his brother as Buck Kessner's Chosen One. Ruby knew it was natural for brothers to feel competition with each other, but it broke her heart to sense that Declan felt like...less.

It was no surprise when he announced he was going to travel for a while. Ruby knew sometimes you had to leave to get an objective view of your home.

"I want you to see the world," Ruby said. "And I am so happy for you. But, remember, there's always someone in Paris or Monaco...or the perfect little vineyard in Italy...who can't wait to get out of their town, too. No place is ever perfect. And even if it's amazing, it isn't always better."

Declan stared at the fire, listening, as Ruby went on.

"Just because Haven is small doesn't mean we're settling for less," Ruby said. "Like you told us when you were younger, some people work all their lives to call a place like this home. And you *always* have a home here, where you're important and seen and loved. I want you to know that, okay? To know that without a doubt."

"Okay, Mom," he'd said, with just enough of a grin for a dimple to form. "I'm not leaving Haven forever. I'm just going on vacation."

Declan didn't come back to the island again until he was twenty-seven.

HE HAD FOUND HE COULD make a decent living with what was dubbed "Taxi Art."

It started as a favor for a cab driver friend he had made in Amsterdam. The little car was old and rusty, and he knew that was why his friend was losing fares. Deck offered to give it a makeover with his bright graffiti art. One taxi led to another. And water taxis, too.

The vehicles that sported his designs made ten times the fares of the others. If two taxis pulled up to a curb or dock, you could guess which one the tourists would choose. And when he was tired of a city or country, Deck would simply move on to the next. He learned to get flailing companies to contract him to makeover their fleet. And he saved up plenty of money to live (simply) wherever he chose.

Deck smoked weed until he passed out. Ate until he needed to diet. He drank and partied and made temporary friends. And was pick-pocketed more than once.

He saw the sun rise over the Swiss Alps, milked an Austrian cow, and attended a fashion show in Milan. He hiked mountains, toured castles, and slept on beaches — and even strolled through a museum or two.

He dated backpacking college girls and aspiring musicians, artists and models and waitresses. One American writer he met in Italy made him believe in love at first sight. Stephanie was her name, but she was only in town for a night.

Of course, he had stayed in touch with his family and friends. Kara and Macy even visited him in Paris. He still owned Cartz, but Mitch Maxwell was running the business just fine.

Ruby and Jack went to see him in Interlaken, Switzerland, where he was playing music for a while at a snowboarders' hostel and bar, The Hot Chili Pepper. And he took his parents to Halstatt, Austria, because he knew his mother would love it there. It was a tiny little sliver of town built on a mountainside that reminded them both of home.

Deck had never forgotten what his mom had said that night by the fire: that no matter how perfect a place might seem, there was someone who wanted to leave it. And he found that to be true, everywhere he went.

It's human nature to want to see what else is out there and compare it to what you have. But never in all of Deck's travels did he find anyplace better than Haven. Prettier? Sure. More lively? You bet. More cultured, more advanced, more exciting? Absolutely. Some had views he could not believe were real. And women who could break his heart. But no place was necessarily *better* than Haven. Just different. And their own kind of amazing.

DECLAN WAS SITTING at a Florence café, about four years into his trip, when he saw a guy with a red ball cap and beard out for an evening jog. He looked, to Deck, like Forrest Gump when he'd set out on that cross-country run. Deck couldn't remember the details, but he knew Forrest had run away from something. His mother's death, perhaps? And he ran and he ran and he ran. Until one day, he simply stopped.

"I'm pretty tired," Forrest announced at the end of that scene. "I think I'll go home now."

Declan finished his beer, paid his tab, and went back to his room to book his plane ticket home. He was ready to go back to Haven and had a whole head full of new ideas: floating tiki bars for Spinnaker's North, called Spin-Offs; a drive-in movie theatre for golf carts; a gourmet sunset cruise with tapas by Alek and live music by Deck; and a micro-brewery hotel where *Sk8ters Haven* used to be. He had visited one in Germany that had beer fridges in the shower! The island could use a winery, too. There was so much more to do.

DECK'S FLIGHT WAS THE last into Haven before they shut the airport down. He thought his mom might be overreacting, letting Paul's paranoia influence her judgment. But it's not like he wanted to leave again anytime soon, so he didn't bother to argue. Declan was just happy to be home.

Then, in January, everything changed. The entire world was shutting down. City by city, country by country, people were locking themselves in their homes to help slow down a deadly disease.

Declan couldn't imagine being anywhere else during this ruthless storm.

And now they were opening their docks? At first, he was furious. How could the government make them do that? But then again, how could they not? Not much surprised Deck anymore. Life rarely went as planned. There was nothing they could do to stop this thing, so he vowed to show Haven to the world in its very best possible light.

"Wake up," he said to the gorgeous brunette sleeping in the bed of his apartment, above the Cartz headquarters on Main. Her hair, a tangled mess of black silk, splayed across her bare chest like lace. Lips, full from sleep and red from kissing, emitted a purring moan. Deck wished he had time to wake her in a much more interesting way.

"Hey," he said, this time followed by a kiss on her silky shoulder. "Wake up."

She opened one eye, then squinted it tight. Rubbing her head, she groaned louder this time. The party for Kara had gone late the night before, and they were both probably still drunk.

Deck hoped everyone was equally buzzed and hadn't seen them leave together.

"What time is it?" she asked, rolling in the other direction.

"Nine," Deck said. "But I have to go set things up for my mom's broadcast. And that reporter's coming at noon."

"Nine o'clock? Shit!" Isabella Flores was up and standing naked inside of two-and-a-half seconds. "Necesito ir a buscar a mi hijo!" *I need to go get my son!*

# ROUNDS BAR

SATURDAY, APRIL 22
12:00 P.M.

"NOW I KNOW HOW INDIANS must have felt when White Man invaded their land," Kade Irish says, standing in his usual spot behind Rounds bar. Everything is set up for his mother's announcement, but no one is allowed in until after the reporter arrives. Which should be in about thirty minutes.

The four Irish siblings have decided they have time for one last drink alone.

Kade fills a pint glass with the Island Ale on tap, takes a sip, then leans elbows-on-the-counter, bartender/therapist style, as he's done for the past five years.

"Native Americans," Georgia says, correcting his 'Indians' faux pas. As the mother of three young children, his older sister insists on political correctness. Even if the kids aren't in the room. Kade can't tell right now if she's being proper or just a smart-ass.

"They were called Indians back then," he says. "And that's not the point. The point is, it feels invasive."

"To me, it feels like The Jungle Book," Declan says. "Only in our story, Man is moving into the jungle instead of Mowgli going to live in the village."

"Are you saying we're the jungle?" Kade asks.

"Well, yeah," Deck says, draining his beer and handing the glass to his brother for a refill. Kade streams another frothy Guinness.

"I mean, sure, Haven is familiar to people from New York, Pennsylvania, Ohio...all the usual suspects." Deck runs a hand through his wavy hair, which is perpetually disheveled. "But people from L.A., Houston, Vegas? To them, we're just some Podunk island in the middle of nowhere."

Some would argue that Declan is the best looking of the four Irish siblings. His lean, tall frame, sharp, sculpted features, and lightest hair by far, make him stand out in family pictures like the celebrity star of an ensemble B-cast. While all four siblings are attractive (think: the prettiest people in your graduating class), Declan just has the "it" factor of someone who's bound for more.

"Well, we're hardly living in thatch huts," Paul says, eyes focused on his own pint of Guinness, which is still ninety percent full. "And I'm sure anyone who chose to come here did their fair share of Haven research. But the photos never do it justice."

Paul is always looking for ways to get their tourist town noticed by the masses. Of the countless ideas he's schemed, of course a pandemic was never imagined. But he will still try to find an angle to make it work to their advantage.

Today, Paul is wearing a pale blue bow tie that looks suspiciously close to a surgical mask, and a crisp, white button-down shirt tucked into his belted jeans. His dark auburn waves have been freshly cut short, an odd display of effort. And his standard black, no-nonsense glasses make him look like the Clark Kent of The Haven Gazette. Paul could probably transform from stuffy to sexy with a simple tweak or two, but it's doubtful he ever will. Paul doesn't care about that.

"I think they will be pleasantly surprised," he says, looking up and around the old pub. "By the rich history of this island and all it has to offer. It could be very good for business when this is all said and done."

The three siblings nod in agreement, appreciating his positive words.

"Assuming we survive this, of course," he says, then takes a small sip of his beer.

"And, pop!" Deck bursts his fingers open as if his hand exploded. "Just like that, he sucks the air right out of the room."

Paul just shakes his head at his brother and resumes staring at his glass. He's nothing at all like his siblings but attends every family event.

"Well, this whole situation reminds me of *The Boy in the Plastic Bubble*," Georgia says before sipping a Cosmo and pulling a sour face. "Eww, more cranberry please."

Kade rolls his eyes and reaches in the cooler for the juice bottle.

"This, coming from the girl who used to drink me under the table with tequila shots," he says with a lopsided grin that reveals one dimple, while topping off his sister's glass.

"You were sixteen. I was twenty-three." Georgia sips, smiles, and approves of her updated martini. "I still had the steel liver of a college student. And *your* drinking career had only just begun."

"Eh, them babies made you soft," Declan says, elbowing his big sis.

"In more ways than one," says Georgia, pinching just a hint of a roll above the waistband of her Lululemons. It's been a year since she gave birth, and she still wants to lose a few pounds, but Georgia is always on-trend, no matter what her size. "Anyway, did Mom ever make you guys watch that movie? *The Boy in the Plastic Bubble*?"

All three Irish brothers shake their heads no.

"Oh, God!" Now it's Georgia's turn for an eyeroll. "It was some movie she had seen when she was a kid and then she found it online. Must've been made in the 70s? About this poor, sick boy, played by a *younnnng* John Travolta, who was born with some kind of immunity disease. And he was put in this isolated room inside the family's house. The walls were soft, clear, pliable plastic, like, well...a *bubble*. His family could only reach in with these horrible giant black gloves, that were attached to the wall, ever since he was a baby."

Her eyes well. And the brothers all exchange looks with flashes of panic.

"Oh my God," Georgia says, hand to heart and then fanning her tear-filled eyes. "Now that I have kids, I realize how awful this movie was!"

Another sip. Big one this time.

"Anyway, he somehow falls in love with his next-door neighbor."

"Through the bubble?" Declan asks, she has his attention now.

"Yes!"

"So they used the big black gloves to...?" Declan raises his eyebrows, inferring his R-rated thoughts.

"No!" Georgia smacks him on the arm. "Omigod! No-o-o! But wait. Maybe they did hold hands that way. And I think they might have kissed through the plastic..."

Declan shoots Kade a look — sly grin, slight nod, wiggling brows — the facial equivalent to *"Bow Chicka Bow Bow."*

"Jesus," Paul says, not above an eyeroll himself. "Just let her finish."

"Yeah, shut up, Deck. Go on, G." Kade leans farther forward in earnest, or he's faking his interest extremely well. It's often hard to tell if the Irish family is being sincere or ironic since they all have the sarcasm gene.

"Thank you," Georgia says. "Anyway, so he spends his entire life living in this bubble. And sometimes in a space suit..."

"A *space* suit?!" Declan asks, eyes shining with humor now, fully entertained. "I have *got* to Google this movie!"

"Shut! Up!" From all three siblings, in perfect unison, after years of practice shushing their baby bro.

"Well, in the end, he finally escapes with Jenny...Genie...something like that. The pretty blonde neighbor. And the credits roll with them walking away together. Outside. I still remember the song. *What would they say if we up and ran away...*"

"So he *dies*?! For the *girl*?" Declan mocks shock and disgust. "That saucy little homewrecker."

"I don't know if he dies," Georgia says. "Maybe he grew out of the disease and they lived happily-ever-after. At least that's what mom told me when I was devastated by the ending. But, anyway, my point is..."

"Finally," says Paul, then takes his biggest sip yet, and uses a napkin to wipe the foam mustache it leaves.

Georgia shoots him some serious side-eye and continues, louder now.

"MY! POINT! IS! WE are the ones in the bubble!"

Her hands fly up, out, and swirl around, illustrating the 'we' — and, they assume, the bubble.

Crunch, Kade's block-headed yellow lab, jerks his head up from the wooden bar floor in ear-perked, awakened alert. Then plunks it again with a thud.

"These fucking so-called 'Survivors' are about to invade our safe, healthy, happy little bubble any freakin' minute!" Georgia's cheeks are red now with alcohol and emotion. "Possibly still carrying the virus, or the secondary stage of it, or whatever. And then passing it on to all of us. Infecting you, me, my kids. This could *kill* Dottie and Frank, you know. And there's not a damn thing we can do about it!"

Silence. The three brothers bounce questioning glances back, forth, and around to each other, like a pinball game of confusion. *What happened? Is she really mad? Weren't we just having fun?*

Each brother wonders who will have the guts to speak next.

In the age-old plight of boys vs. girls, men vs. women, Mars vs. Venus, they have never been able to figure out their sister. Being the only female in their family besides their mom, and the second oldest sibling, Georgia's role was ever-changing. She alternated between bossy and babyish, fearless and fragile, funny and sensitive, angry and calm...often all in the same day.

Georgia grew up strong, feisty, and smart. She learned early on that in order to stand out in this testosterone zoo, she needed to mix it up. And sometimes she had to roar.

It's Declan who braves the first response.

"Well," he says, raising his glass to take another sip. "We could always wear space suits!"

Paul emits a rare burst of a chuckle that sounds like the combination of a stifled sneeze and a goose honk. Which makes Georgia smile. And tensions release.

Shoulders relax. Breaths are let out. The four siblings finish the rest of their drinks and give the glasses to Kade just in time to pose picture-perfect when their parents walk through the door with a cute, brunette, smiling stranger.

"PAUL. GEORGIA. KADE. DECLAN." Ruby presents each child with an open palm as she says their name in the same order she has for years, and then waves her hand back toward the young woman. "This is Grace Dawson from the TV-6 NBC News out of Traverse City, Michigan. Ms. Dawson, this is my family."

"Hi," they all say together, with friendly waves and welcoming smiles, except for Declan who only glares.

"Stephanie?" He says, first shocked, then his face opens up to a smile — all dimples, and blue eyes, and trouble.

"Hanson?" She asks, eyes wide, while the rest of her face doesn't know what to do.

Ruby raises her eyebrows and looks between the two.

"Stephanie?" She questions first to the reporter by her side.

"Stephanie Grace Dawson." The flustered young woman is trying, and failing miserably, to regain her composure. "I go by Grace now. For work."

"Hanson?" Ruby asks her son, Declan Hanson Irish, whose cheeks are reddening now.

Ruby looks around at the rest of her family, who are all beaming glares at each other like a game of laser tag. They had all heard about a Stephanie when Declan came home on Thanksgiving. She was the only girl from Europe that he'd described by name.

It was Stephanie, Georgia remembers, that made Deck believe in love at first sight. She wonders if her mom recalls this. And can see, by her smirk, that Ruby does.

It's Kade who breaks the silence next as he pushes the tapper back on the beer he'd been pouring.

"Well then!" Kade's own dimpled, mischievous smile makes him look remarkably like Deck — and a fair amount of trouble himself. He sets the pint glass on the counter and slides it toward the now red-faced Stephanie Grace.

"Welcome to Haven!"

# THE BROADCAST

SATURDAY, APRIL 22
1:00 p.m.

HELLO, MY NAME IS RUBY Irish. I am the mayor of Haven-on-the-Lake, a small island of 3.8 square miles, located in Lake Erie, which is bordered by Michigan, Ohio, Pennsylvania, New York, and Canada.

We are a popular tourist destination for people all over the world in the months from May through mid-October. When the season is over, we close our docks and can only be accessed by plane. Therefore, our 183 full-time residents rarely come and go in the winter. And very few seasonal residents or tourists come to Haven this time of year.

When news of the virus in Asia was first released in November, before the American government seemed to think it was a threat, we made the decision on Haven to close our airport Thanksgiving Day. It was a concern of several citizens here that this could be a global pandemic, and we chose to isolate ourselves.

Only our resident pilot, Captain Gregory Finnegan, left the island for essential supplies. We arranged for supplies to be loaded on the plane without Captain Finnegan coming in personal contact with anyone on the mainland. And then the supplies were unpackaged and sterilized before they were distributed here. You could say the captain was sterilized, too, with a shower and change of clothes before he even left the airport.

Not long after the new year, as all of you now well know, countries all over the world imposed their own protective guidelines in response to the global pandemic. You are all, by now, familiar with social distancing, sheltering-in-place, and, in some cities, complete lockdowns. However, because we had no contact with anyone else since November, we considered Haven as one common, united place, and have sheltered together here. Our entire city has, thankfully, remained healthy, safe, and protected from this horrible disease.

Because Haven-on-the-Lake residents have online businesses, remote positions in mainland companies, and other sources of income, we were fully prepared to remain closed to the public for the upcoming tourist season. And next year's season, too, if that would protect our residents' lives. This decision was fully supported by part-time residents and property owners, out of respect for those who hold down the fort six months of the year by maintaining their buildings and businesses and keeping their belongings safe. Also, there are several elderly and vulnerable residents living full-time on Haven, who are the living legacy and very history of our beautiful, time-honored town. And we are especially concerned for them.

We have recently been informed by government officials that our efforts to remain sheltered in Haven are not within the authority of myself or the popular vote. And we will no longer be allowed to isolate and protect ourselves from the rest of the world.

By order of the President of the United States, Haven-on-the-Lake, as of one week from today, will be deemed the first official Immunity Community for the Survivors of this vicious virus.

This community is being created in response to the requests, demands, and protests of the Survivors Freedom Alliance: a large, growing group of individuals who have recovered from the virus and now feel they should be exempt from virus-related restrictions, and free to resume life and business as they did before the illness struck.

Therefore, a selection of 980 individuals, enough to fill the lodging currently available, will arrive on the island in stages, heretofore known as waves.

These vetted and authorized individuals, heretofore known as Survivors, will have met several extensive medical requirements that deem them as recovered, non-contagious, and virus-free. And they will continue to be tested.

The Survivors chosen for this community have been carefully screened and selected with very specific criteria to meet a variety of goals. This criteria includes, but is not limited to professions, talents, and expertise that are needed to create an optimal, well-rounded, cohesive society that is productive as well.

Three of the Haven's largest facilities will be converted to employ Survivors to produce surgical-grade protective gowns for healthcare workers, fabric masks to meet growing public demand, and hand sanitizer for selected distribution. This is welcome news to many in light of the record-breaking unemployment percentages that are also plaguing our country.

This, we hope, will raise the morale of America as a whole, and help us see beyond the limitations and implications of this disease.

In that same spirit, and because Survivors are deemed non-contagious, there will be **no virus-related social restrictions in regard to human interaction.**

Survivors will be permitted to live their lives as we all did in 2019. There will be no social distancing requirements. Masks will not be required. Restaurants, bars, and other business will be allowed to serve at full capacity. There will be concerts, movies, sporting events, religious services, and large social gatherings equivalent to those that existed before this virus took over the world.

Because of this, and for obvious reasons, we cannot risk anyone else coming onto our island who is not a confirmed Survivor.

By my request, the government has committed to provide maximum protection to Haven-on-the-Lake so that no other individuals besides those authorized and approved will be able to enter our borders. With the help of the military and private security companies, all docks and access points will be guarded by water. Drones and satellite images will provide aerial observation. No watercrafts will be permitted within the restricted boundaries and limits that the security teams deem safe and required.

As for the health, safety, and status of our current Haven residents: It has been stated by government and medical officials that the eligible Survivors are of minimal threat to the current residents of Haven-on-the-Lake, and, therefore, the current Haven residents are permitted to stay in their homes.

They have also been given the option to relocate to the mainland, with small compensation by the government for their...*inconvenience.*

The main reasoning behind interacting unexposed residents with virus survivors is a positive and optimistic one: As our country comes together again, hopefully in the near future, there will be people who survived the disease in contact with those who have never been exposed. When neither party has an active infection, then supposedly neither party can catch it. The interaction of Haveners with Survivors will hopefully set an example that we all can, and will, survive the future of this disease together.

That being said, I would be remiss in not admitting that I do have many concerns for the safety of Haven residents.

After painstakingly extracting honest answers from the powers-that-be, it cannot be stated, without a shadow of a doubt, that all Survivors are non-contagious.

Testing of both the virus and antibodies has not been failproof.

The virus has been known to exhibit what is called, in layman's terms, "peek-a-boo symptoms," in which patients may look and feel fully recovered. And even test negative for the virus. Only to suffer a relapse, days or weeks later.

Also, there is still a possibility of secondary illness arising in individuals who have had the virus, which could make them contagious again.

Therefore, these individuals do, in fact, pose a threat to the citizens of Haven-on-the-Lake — an island that could have isolated itself for months, even years, from any contact with the virus at all.

However, by order of the President of the United States, and I quote: "We cannot wait and see what this virus may or may not do going forward. We have to get our economy up and running again. We have to connect as a country, and as human beings. Therefore, risks need to be taken. And since the risks are slim that Survivors of the virus remain contagious, they are deemed safe to interact with those who have not had the disease, as well as those who are currently infected. They are, for all intents and purposes, considered immune to the virus. Therefore, they are safe to resume their lives as normal. And they are much-needed examples of resilience during this bleak and trying time. Successfully uniting Survivors with the current residents of Haven — and allowing the rest of the world to see this happen — will be a beacon of hope for our country: that we will resume, revive, and thrive once again. Even better than we did before."

Therefore, although I still have deep concern for the citizens of our town, I am announcing today that Haven-on-the-Lake is the first official Immunity Community as of Saturday, April 29$^{th}$.

It is my hope that we will accomplish the President's goal to be a beacon of hope to all of you.

We are proud to serve as an example of a thriving economy, vibrant social scene, and resilient human beings. And we are excited for you to meet our town.

We are a long-standing community of faith, loyalty, and strength, armed with the history, endurance, and valiance of many survivors before. And we will do our best to rise to this, and any future challenges, that the world may bring our way.

We also hope to serve as inspiration and motivation to you, our fellow Americans, and to the rest of the world, to keep doing *your* part by adhering to local rules and regulations to help slow the spread, stay healthy, and overcome this virus once and for all.

In the coming days, you will see Haveners and Survivors unite as one peaceful and unified community. And we hope to welcome you, in person, to our island very soon.

God bless.

Stay safe.

Be well.

Be the first to read each new installment
of the Haven-on-the-Lake series
as soon as they're publisher-perfect!
Sign up today at
quinleydixon.com[1]

VISIT QUINLEY DIXON ONLINE
instagram.com/quinleydixonauthor[2]
facebook.com/quinley.dixon[3]
And join the Facebook discussion group:
Quinley Dixon's Quinning Team[4]

---

1. https://www.quinleydixon.com/
2. https://www.instagram.com/quinleydixonauthor/
3. https://www.facebook.com/quinley.dixon/
4. https://www.facebook.com/groups/2602642790023261

## ABOUT THE AUTHOR

Quinley Dixon began her career in journalism and advertising until she landed her dream job at one of the "big two" greeting card companies where she wrote nearly 20,000 cards for just about every occasion. She has also been a pro blogger, content creator, and public speaking instructor, but always had a novel in the works. She holds a couple of Bachelor of Arts degrees from Michigan State University and lives in Rochester Hills, Michigan, with her two teenage sons, two dogs, and several geese and deer families that frequent their yard. But she dreams of living on an island with a golf cart as her car.

This is her first published novel of many more to come.

Find out more at Quinley Dixon's site[5].

---

5. https://quinleydixon.com/

## ACKNOWLEDGMENTS

Thank you to my editor and proofreader, Terri Hersey, who was my first visitor to Haven-on-the-Lake and motivated me to share it with the world. Hold on to that ferry ticket! You will forever have the first VIP pass to the island.

Thank you to Pat Kotkowski who listened to my unofficial audio version of the chapters, said "Aww" in just the right places, and told me to keep reading, and writing, more.

Thank you to my lifelong loyal, loving, and laugh-out-loud funny Warrior tribe who not only celebrated with me the day I typed THE END, but has encouraged, supported, and loved me fiercely forever. We are a family that we created ourselves and I honestly would not be the person I am today without each and every one of you for exactly who you are.

To the family I was born into, thank you for dubbing me as the creative one for as long as I can remember and believing in every artistic dream I ever had. You are the reason why it comes natural for me to "write family" because of our own seamless dynamics, natural banter, and no-matter-what acceptance and love.

Thank you to my Spartan crew and travel buddies who taught me how friendships can just get better and deeper and more real over the years. You will always be the authentic inspiration for the girlfriends in my books.

To my Jeremiah Girls who all agree it takes village...thank you for being mine.

Tuesdays With Amy! You've been telling me for years to write my book (and another and another) and here it is! Thank you for being incredible examples of fearless women, talented authors, and super-cool human beings.

To the real Ruby, who was all kinds of amazing, I was hoping to get this out by your 100$^{th}$ birthday and I did! Wish you were here to celebrate. But I know you're cheering me on up there...barefoot, in your shorts, with a Pepsi in hand.

Continued prayers for those affected by COVID-19. May you find support and resilience during this time and may we all find a haven from this storm.

And THANK YOU TO INFINITY to my boys, Cooper and Dawson, who show me every single day that it's not only possible to get what you pray, try, and hope for...but that dreams can come true even better than we could possibly imagine. You are both awesome sons, good guys, and hilarious people.

And you make me happy and proud every day.

Made in the USA
Middletown, DE
16 August 2020